‫‫‫‫‫‫‫‫‫‫ OUTSIDE ‫
THE GATES

OUTSIDE THE GATES
THE GATES

BY MOLLY GLOSS

ATHENEUM   1986   NEW YORK

Atheneum
Macmillan Publishing Company
866 Third Avenue, New York, NY 10022

Type set by Maryland Linotype Composition, Baltimore, Maryland
Printed and bound by Fairfield Graphics, Fairfield, Pennsylvania
Designed by Annie Alleman

10 9 8 7 6 5 4 3 2 1

Library of Congress Cataloging-in-Publication Data

Gloss, Molly.   Outside the gates.

"An Argo book."
SUMMARY: Vren, exiled into the dark forest outside
the Gates, finds a new life with a friendly weather-
worker, until their gentle existence is disrupted by a
spellbinder misusing his power.
[1. Fantasy] I. Title.
PZ7.G49Ou   1986   [Fic] 85-28740
ISBN 0-689-31275-X

For Ben

ᘒᘒᘒᘒᘒᘒ CONTENTS ᘒ

ᓚᓚᓚᓚᓚᓚᓚᓚᓚ OUTSIDE ᓚ THE GATES

ⓐⓐⓐⓐⓐⓐⓐⓐ 1 ⓐ A SONG FOR GOING ON

The boy thought his heart would stop from the thunder sound the Gates made as they closed behind him. But he did not cry. He was more afraid than that. He only stood very still and small, and when the booming echo had slid down the pass into the forest, the boy still stood. He was alone and shut out. The high black doors of the Gates filled up the pass behind him, rising sheer and smooth to the rim of the plain.

There was a stream near where the boy stood. It ran out from under the edge of the Gates themselves, down between the rocks and finally out of sight in the darkness under the trees. The great forest, stretching out from there to the edges of the sky, was called the UnderReach.

The boy knew the 'Reach was the home of giants and monsters—other children had told him. If any people lived there, beneath the trees, they would be Shadowed, for the boy's people had ever lived on the high, open plain, close to the sun, and only a man or a woman or a child who was found to be Shadowed was put out to live in the unknown darknesses of the UnderReach.

The boy was afraid to go down into the woodland where the giants and the Shadowed people lived. He stayed where he was, near the loud little river, among the rocks at the bottom of the Gates. He waited. At night he cried to be let in, but in the gray daylight he did not cry at all. He only lay there dully in the wind and cold, waiting, among the white bones of other people who had waited.

On the third day, two small rock sheep came up from the trees and watched him. Finally, boldly, they came to lick the salt from his skin. Their company and their brave faces gave him a little bravery. When they went back down to the woodland, he took his troublesack and slowly followed them.

He had not, before this, stood under the roof of a forest. There were, here and there, solitary whip-leaf trees that grew on the plain; and once, when he had been still a very small child, the boy had stood beneath the branches of one of those trees, holding onto his father's hand and staring for comfort out to the wide grassland and the big sky and the far flat line of the horizon. In the forest of the UnderReach where the sheep now led him, there was no horizon. The sky, through the tops of the trees, became quickly distant, broken in pieces and scattered. But he could not stay among the rocks, among the bones. And the Gates, at least, stood up so high he could see them every time he looked back that whole day and the next. So he kept on, following the sheep at first, and later going on alone, into the forest.

It rained. Under the trees there was a slow, steady leaking. Slowly, steadily, the boy himself grew wet. The yellow dog's-wool cape that had been in his troublesack let in the rain through its loose weave. There was a metal strike-fire in the sack, and a thin-bladed knife. With the knife he shaved little bits of tinder, but his small, stiff hands could not move quickly enough: Each time he struck a spark, the rain put it out. So he was cold, too, and after that, sick. He lay on the puddled ground, with the wet cape pulled close, and shook.

The Gatekeeper, as he had given the boy his trouble-sack, had seemed to say by the look on his face, *You see, we are not pitiless.* But afterward the boy had seen the rotted rags of troublesacks among the bones at the bottom of the Gates, and he thought he would die now, himself, holding the strike-fire and the knife in his fist. He thought perhaps all the Shadowed people shut outside the Gates had died thus, alone and cold and afraid, and that after all, there were only giants and monsters alive in the forest of the UnderReach.

So he cried out loud when he saw that someone had come silently to stand above him.

And still he cried when he saw it was a man, neither giant nor monstrous, who stood looking down on him. The man did not speak, he only stood and stared at the boy, but he had a bony, angry-looking face, eyes hidden below fierce brows, and wild red hair sticking out from beneath a pointed hat. And he was Shadowed, surely, for there were no other people known to live in the 'Reach.

The boy had still a child's notion of the shapes a Shadow could take: He imagined the man might turn him into a calf or a goat and then kill and eat him. So he lay helplessly under the man's steady stare, and he cried.

Rain dribbled from the wide cone of the man's hat down onto the boy's face. Then the man did make a small movement of anger—a shrugging of his shoulder, a pushing-away with one hand. But it was the rain, not the boy, that had annoyed him. The boy still heard its whispering sound, still saw it like a curtain in the far trees, but now the rain no longer fell where the man stood, nor where the boy lay. The man had simply, by moving his hand, made a dry place for them both, in the wet day.

In a while, when the boy's tears had gone dry too, the man said slowly, "They have put you out of the Gates, have they." The voice was unlike the frightening face.

There was no anger in it. There was simply a heaviness, like sorrow. Then in a moment he said, "Was put out young, myself," as if it were a surprise to him, something he had not thought of before now.

The boy began to cry again, but not this time from fear; and in a while, without saying anything more, the man squatted down and gathered the boy up gently in his arms as if he were not a lean-legged child, instead a baby with legs too wobbly for walking.

The man, Rusche, had a house that was made like a weaver-bird's nest, of small sticks and grass and mud, with a rounded roof and slanted sides and a small low hole for a door. He had not put it high on a limb as a weaver-bird would, but instead had built it on a hillside, under big old teba trees, so the thick boughs of the trees would help to keep the rain off the roof. If the tebas could do the work of keeping the house dry, he was glad to let them.

Sometimes, though, in that first autumn Rusche and the boy were together, rain fell hard right through the arms of the trees. Sometimes a wind flapped the clouds like sheets of cloth. Then Rusche—with a look in his face that was both cross and ashamed—would set a warm little whirlwind by the doorhole to keep the cold from blowing in. Or he would thin the rain so it fell fine and dry as dust through the smokehole in their roof. And by such homely weather-working, Rusche—and now the boy, Vren—lived most of the time snug and dry.

They were sometimes hungry. In that fall when Vren first came, the ceiling and walls of the little house were lined with stores the weather-worker had put by for winter. He had bunches of dried chai and tea-moss, baskets of po nuts, long braids of elbec bulbs. And the stiff, dark bodies of tayfish and brush-rabbits, smoked until they were dry and hard.

The boy ate the chai, in a salty thin broth, and he liked a pudding the man made by crushing elbec with a stone and cooking it thick. But he could not eat the dead animals.

He had long ago learned to pretend, and he did that now, carefully. Yet each time Rusche ate of meat—and the boy pretended to eat of it—the man looked round at the boy silently. It was a look that stopped Vren's breath. His own people had taken notice, slowly, of uneaten meat, and then more quickly afterward they had become aware of the grass snakes and the owl and the old mole Vren had secretly befriended. And though his father drove off the snakes and sealed every mole's burrow with salt and stones, and though his mother held his chin and fed him the owl's own flesh, someone by then had already whispered "Shadowed," and he had been put out of the Gates. Now, the look in Rusche's face made him remember the darkness that had been in the faces of his people, in the days before he was put out—and at night now he cried, with his fist against his mouth to keep the sound in.

The man, through those first days together, only watched the boy silently from under his fierce red brows. Then finally, straightforward, he said, "You speak the languages of beasts, is it?"

The boy ducked his head. No one inside the Gates had given a name to his Shadow, as the man did now. He had to think a little, to know what answer he could make.

"No," he said in a low voice, without looking at Rusche. Then, because the man waited, and continued to watch him, he thought of something more to say. "So much of their language is Smell," he said shyly.

Rusche, in a moment, made a wordless grunting sound. The boy could not tell whether it meant understanding, or doubt.

Afterward, though, the man put all of the meat out of the house. He buried or burned it, or perhaps he left it on the frosted ground for the hungry blue ravens and the spotted wolverines. The boy and the man ate carefully of what was left, growing thin together over the cold season. Vren slept, finally, without those dead animals in the darkness of the house there with him. And finally he saw, below the man's great, angry-seeming brows, eyes that were green and patient and kind.

In the winter, when ice was in the river, the boy and the man walked to a place the man called the Cat's Tail.

"It will be frozen now," Rusche said, as if that were reason enough for going.

The boy walked the whole way there on his own legs, lifting and setting his snowshoes down in the tracks of the man without often falling behind. They stood and looked at how beautiful the falls were, frozen, like a rope of white glass in the cold—and it was, after all, reason enough for going.

Afterward, without speaking of tiredness, Rusche simply carried the boy home on his shoulders.

In a hoarse, plain voice, the man sang a wordless rhyme. "A song for going on," Rusche said, and he sang, "Tey lee fettle, mey ree lettle, lo, by, lo."

The boy rode with his cold hands pushed inside the neck edge of the man's cape and his cold cheeks burrowed in the man's thick red hair. He even slept a little, rocked by the man's steady stride. From the edge of sleep, it seemed to him that he heard no walker's chant, instead a cradle song.

In that winter, when the wind drifted the snow in

high swells, Vren made caves with long tunnels joining them together. He and the minks and the big white snow skunks played games of go-seek in those cold bluish burrows. Sometimes he imagined he could dig a snow tunnel all the way beneath the Gates, and climb out on the other side, on the high plain where his people lived. In that daydream they were glad to find him again. He imagined that he had, after all, only been lost, and not put out. They set their robes about his shoulders and let him sit in the best place in the kin-house, close beside his family's stove. His mother brought him milk-sweetened tea in a big metal cup, and afterward held him close and sang softly until he slept.

In the spring, in the time of tiny green buds, the boy and the weather-worker went up to a place the man called the Basket Meadows, to dig the sweet bulbs of elbec and gather their long thick leaves. The night sky over those meadows seemed very clear and close, like the sky over the plain. Though they did not know the true names of the stars, Rusche and Vren lay on their backs and looked for shapes of their own in the aimless, endless star field—a seed-comb here, a hat or a kettle there. Afterward, the boy painted the shapes and names on a circle of teba-cloth, and he rolled up that star chart carefully, meaning to save it.

He had found, all alone, the shapes of the yellow bear

and the short-tailed hawk. He thought he and the man might be able to name the whole sky, little by little, if they were patient. It was only some time afterward that he remembered his daydream and wondered whether his family would come looking for him, to take him home, before he and Rusche had finished naming the stars.

In that spring, when the leaves came out on all the hardwood trees, the boy climbed high among the houses of the black squirrels and the woodhole birds, and they played with him their games of drop-cone and who-sees. From there in the trees he could see the sheer edge of the tableland standing up, bluish in the distance. Sometimes, if he stared hard enough, and if the sky was very clear and light, he even thought he could see the sun flashing off the smooth blackness of the Gates.

He liked to look toward that place where the plain began. He imagined, if he let loose his toehold in the tree, he could take flight like an archeagle and glide on the long wind over the Gates to the people on the other side. He imagined his mother weeping as she held him, and his father carrying him home high and proudly on his shoulders, singing a loud song of celebration.

But sometimes, in that daydream, he only swooped in low and angry over the heads of the people and raked his long eagle's talons in their hair. Then he would see all their faces jerking up, staring at him in surprise and fear. Sometimes, as in the other daydream, his mother wept.

In the summer, from the time of ripe strawberries, the boy and the man began to spend many of their days far afield. They hunted mushrooms and red onions, berries of many kinds, and the soft, peppery new shoots of salset. And from time to time, on their far walking, they came on the lonely house of a neighbor or the camp of a wanderer.

The people of the UnderReach lived, nearly all of them, alone. They made no villages and few families. "They have no pride," Rusche said in a rough voice, as if that were reason enough. Vren, without understanding the word, understood the meaning. He had, after all, not been lost, but cast out.

Rusche would often take the boy's hand and stand at the edge of a camp, waiting until they were seen, and then waiting again for welcome. If a tea-bowl was carefully tipped and spilled on the ground, they went away without a word. But if the bowl was filled up high enough for sharing, and the boiling-rocks put to heat on the fire, then they came slowly in. Rusche and the other person would sit opposite one another and shyly speak their little bits of news: a death they had heard of, a new house built or a house left suddenly empty, a man or woman met on a trail. They shared, also, the small,

---

important ways each of them had learned to live in the forest of the UnderReach: this tree's leaf or that plant's flower they had found fit for food or for comfort.

Often, wanderers spoke of the landmarks of the 'Reach as they were known in small ways to each of them, so the boy learned the edges of that vast forest: a high white line of mountains, a stormy lake without a far shore, a broad ironwood thicket where no animal lived. He wondered if anyone had ever gone outside the borders of the UnderReach—and he wondered, if he left the 'Reach, if he might not be able to leave his Shadow at its edge.

Seldom, and vaguely, someone spoke of the tableland, or the people who lived there on the high plain, or the Gates that guarded those people from Shadows. Then Vren listened in silence and dreadful curiosity. But the Gates had been built so long ago that it seemed no one now alive, in the forest or on the plain, remembered the true reason. Inside the Gates there had been only old tales, as vivid and terrifying and inexplicable as nightmares. And outside the Gates it seemed there were only old habits, of fear and of shame.

In the long, still days of that summer, when the air stood thick and hot under the trees, the boy swam in the river. There was a ring-tailed otter who lived in the reeds a little way upstream, and often the boy and the otter

would dive from high rocks straight into the deepest part
of the water, or they would race one another hard upstream against the current.

Rusche had named the river White Stone, but the boy
imagined it was the same one that ran out from under
the Gates, the little stream those people called the
Tilseth. He wondered if he might be strong enough,
by now, to swim all the way up the river to that place
where the White Stone River ran under the Gates and
became the Tilseth. Later, in a dream, he became a
tayfish and swam under the edge of the Gates and up the
rocks of the pass into the clear brightness and wind of
the plain.

In that dream, he stepped out of the water among the
long stone kin-houses of his own village. No one would
speak his name. Their looks made him feel afraid and
dangerous and powerful. Their faces were all white,
and he could smell fear on their bodies. He could not
tell which of the terrible, frightened faces might be his
father's. He woke, sweating, and heard the sound he
must have made, the little cry. But Rusche's hand was
touching his wrist gently, silently, in the darkness, and
in a while the last of the dream leaked out into the night.

For a while, when the fall came round again, the rain
fell straight and fine and silent, as if it would not ever
be finished. Then the boy and the man spent whole days

inside their house, playing games of Seven-Sticks, weaving rain capes from the inner bark of the teba tree, braiding sandals from the dried leaves of elbec. Rusche kept a long teba-string with knots in it to mark the days and the seasons; and one day, holding the boy's small hands in his own large, freckled ones, he showed him how to tie a knot that would mark Vren's first year outside the Gates. Then he let go the boy's hands so he might tie that knot himself.

Afterward, the man made a sweet, wet cake of honey and blackberries and flour ground from seeds of wild blue rice.

"It has rained for seven days," he said gruffly, as if that were the reason for sharing a sweet treat.

By that fall, the red-back wolf pups born in the spring had grown out of babyness. When the fall's weather went dry and windy, Vren spent three days with them. It felt good to be able to wrestle roughly with someone and play serious games of hunt-and-ambush in the thick brush below the den. And he liked to feel himself part of that big family, to share in their noisy, open love. In the darkness, the boy raised his voice in high wailing star-song with the pups and the parents and a young uncle who had become his particular friend. He even slept in the wolves' small den, curled up tightly with the others so there should have been no room for loneliness.

In a while, though, he found he was homesick.

From the ridge behind the den he stood and watched the great flights of gray fisher-geese. From that high place, on the clear days, the line of the tableland seemed very close, as if one might walk to the foot of the plain in an afternoon. But the boy did not look toward the Gates. For a while now, he had only seen the faces of those people in his dreams.

He watched the geese. Then he bumped noses with each of the wolves, in thanks and farewell, and he went home again to Rusche.

⚭⚭⚭ 2 ⚭ THE EMPTY HOUSE

In the fall, soon after the boy had tied his sixth year-knot in Rusche's string, he went down the valley of the White Stone River to take wool from the yellow bears. There were several families of them who grazed the lower end of the valley in that season. Every year, Vren came and spent a few days of the fall camping among them. He combed burrs and ticks from their coats, and then, as they stood or lay patiently, he cropped the long, coarse wool from their shoulders. Their hair would lengthen again, and thicken, before the cold weather had set in. And the bears' wool, woven over hearts of teba-string, made a warmer, tougher legging than the ones Rusche had used to make all of teba-cloth.

The boy liked being among the bears. They were calm and easily pleased. There was not much cleverness in their small, close-set eyes, but Vren saw peace there, and dignity. He spent four or five days with them, following as they wandered up and down the valley, harvesting blackberries and cattail stems and mustard leaves, through the long orange afternoons. Then he put in his old troublesack the few things he had brought with him, took up the big light bundle of the bears' wool, and he went off home again.

It was a good day for walking, cool and cloudy. The boy and Rusche, coming and going from their house to the berry fields, had over the years worn a thin trail along the banks of the White Stone River, and the boy followed it easily. It crossed and recrossed the water, choosing the open bank wherever windfallen trees or rocks or thickets stood in the way.

In the shallows foxweed sometimes found sunny places to grow, and there the boy could see the thick seed pods already ripe. He went on by them. He and Rusche could come up this path in a day or two with a basket and a seed comb and harvest what the deer had not found. He did not want to stop for foxweed now. He was suddenly impatient for Rusche, as he always was when he had started home after being away. He went upriver steadily, wading across the water and across again, following the path. He took off his leggings and carried them in his troublesack so the cold clear water splashed his bare calves. He let the water run right in and out the open sides of his elbec sandals.

Rusche seemed always uncomfortable at leave-takings and home-comings, and that had made the boy shy of them also. It was his habit to come in as if he had not gone away. He would set down his troublesack and begin at once to help the man beat out a spruce cloth or weave the flat strips of cattail leaves to make a mat—and it was only from the corner of his eye that he saw, each time, Rusche's slight, slow smile welcoming him.

Now, when he came up from the riverbank toward the high tebas where the house sat, what he felt was not shyness. It was stronger and stranger than that, an unquiet that blew through him like a wind. All at once he became unwilling to go the last short way to the house. He stood just beyond sight of it and took a breath, but the dark thing he felt only settled in his chest. He stood a long time, waiting, without quite knowing for what he waited. And finally, though he had none of his breath or his heart back, he went on again, slowly, until he could see the house.

It squatted as ever, under the low branches of the tebas, but it was clearly empty and cold. There were bits of stepped-on food and broken sticks on the ground in front of the doorhole. The house Rusche had built with his own hands looked now sad and poorly made, as if no one could ever have lived snugly there. The boy stood where he was and stared.

"Hello," he said after a while, and was ashamed to hear his voice sounding thin and afraid.

"Haloo-oo!" he said again, in a loud shout that went out into the trees and then down into the cold center of him. There was no answer. He had known there would not be.

The house had been like a squirrel's nest, its walls and ceiling hung with their harvest of summer and fall. Now all of the food and most of the tools were gone. Only a few jumbled things had been left behind. The boy and Rusche had split and shredded a pile of red teba bark, and the soft unwoven strings lay stepped on. There was a broken digging stick on the ground, too, with an old wooden seed-beater and a berry basket with a hole to mend, and things without workaday use: the boy's old star chart, a carven set of Seven-Sticks, and Rusche's long calendar string, tangled among the ashes of his last fire. The boy straightened the string carefully and counted knots. There was no knot marking this day, and none for the day before.

The boy walked up and down both banks of the river, from the Cat's Tail to the Big Turn. He walked slowly, looking for a print of Rusche's foot in the mud or the grass. There was nothing that seemed clear enough to follow. He went along each of the smaller paths they had made, to mushroom beds and patches of mint and fields of elderberry. He climbed his high lookout tree and stared over the woods until his eyes burned. He used a long stick to poke into thorny bushes and into boggy places where he knew the mud could swallow something big as a man. He even dove down into the deep places in the river, swimming slowly through the cold water with his eyes wide open.

At night when the light was gone, he went back to the empty house. There was a firestick in his troublesack but he did not break it to make a fire. He lay down alone in the cold darkness and slept little. He was careful not to think of Rusche. Instead, carefully, he thought of the landmarks of the UnderReach, drawing on the darkness of his closed eyes a chart as fine and complete as the star chart he and the man had once made together. This one, though, was a map of all the places he had already searched, and all the others where he might yet find Rusche.

The sleep he got was filled with broken pieces of frightening dreams.

On the second day he went all the way up to the elbec fields at the Basket Meadows, half a day's walk. He went round them, calling Rusche's name out loud. And then he walked slowly back down from there alone.

On the second night, when he shut his eyes, he could no longer draw a map against the darkness. All the places he knew had been searched. When he saw Rusche's face behind his eyelids, he opened his eyes again and stared at the two stars showing through the smokehole in the roof.

In a while, in silence and darkness, he felt the wolf come and stand in the doorway of the house. It was

Trim, the uncle, who was, after Rusche, the first and best of Vren's friends. The wolf made a sound, a growl so faint it was like a cat's purr, and then he came in and lay beside the boy. The boy put his face against Trim's rough coat, his arms around the thick neck. He had not cried for Rusche yet, but now that Trim was there he did cry a little. He felt better afterward, as if he had taken off something that was too tight.

The boy knew at once that the parents had stayed behind with their spring-born litter. They had given Trim, who was unmarried and youngest of the three, the charge of their friend. Vren did not wonder at all how the wolves had found out his need. He was sure he would have known theirs.

In the morning, in a cold gray light, Trim went over many of the places the boy had already searched. He kept his muzzle close to the ground, smelling for Rusche as Vren had looked for his footprint.

The boy knew there must be many old scent-marks around their house, so he waited patiently, sitting on his heels, while the wolf nosed about. After a short time, Trim lifted up his head and looked straight at the boy and then turned and started off. He led Vren over the hill and into the long canyon behind it, where there were leafless po nut trees and the sweet smell of the hot springs. The boy had looked along that path all the way to its end the day before, but he followed the wolf. Past the po nuts, the trail was dim, seldom used. There was no neighbor's house known to lie that way, only sparse bushes of thimbleberries and, in the spring, spider-leaf and thistles. In a short time, the paths worn by Rusche and Vren dribbled out. Still the wolf went on, along the trails of deer and bear.

When they had gone beyond the edges of land the boy knew, Vren fell behind a little and finally he stopped. He squatted on the ground and shut his eyes.

He had learned, long before, that there were no monsters, no giants, here in the UnderReach, only a few poor cast-off people living in solitary shame. But Vren felt there must be some fearful, black thing hidden in each of them, for he remembered the look in his father's face, and in the face of the Gatekeeper, and he remembered the old nightmare tales from his childhood inside the Gates. He had waited and watched for evil in himself and in Rusche, as a mouse watches for the shadow of a hawk, and now he wondered if Rusche's going was a sign of it. For a moment, with his eyes closed, the boy felt as he had a long time ago, looking down from the pass into the dark, endless forest. He wanted to stay where he was, very still and small.

In a little while, Trim made a sound of impatience. The boy opened his eyes and saw the wolf waiting, looking back. The red fur along his shoulders stood up in a high ruff against the chill. His eyes were yellow and steady.

Slowly the boy pulled his troublesack to his shoulder and followed the wolf. He was careful not to look back along the narrow trail that went back to the empty house.

Just at dusk they came to a little lake without inlet or outlet, a pond the boy named Rain Lake. It was the first water since they had left the White Stone River. Trim drank from it and lay down on the shore. The boy set down his sack and unfastened his leggings and waded bare-legged in the shallows, amid the thin stems of wild rice. When he looked up again, Trim was gone. Like the boy, the wolf hunted his meal.

The boy made a little fire and boiled and ate the rice. It was very dark by then, and the air felt cold and damp. He took Rusche's calendar string from his troublesack and tied a day-knot in it. Then he tied the ends of the string together, looped it several times and hung it round his neck inside his shirt. That done he drew his cape close and lay down beside the small flame.

His eyes burned, but he could not sleep without Trim. So finally, tiredly, he could not help but think of Rusche. He let himself imagine that, for the second time in his life, he had been cast away. He imagined that the man had taken all their things and willingly left the little round house they had lived in together for six years. He imagined him packing baskets and sacks, stowing every-thing carefully so he could carry it all from his shoulders and on his back and at his hips. He could even see the man's face, looking angry as he ever seemed to, with his great brows hiding his eyes. But he could not see the man's hands. When he tried to imagine Rusche's freckled, big-knuckled hands tossing aside the star chart, or the long calendar string with, now, six of the boy's knots in it, he could not.

After that, with a kind of fierce anger and joy, he imagined monsters and giants, and the several different ways he and Trim would find to rescue Rusche from them.

೭ ೭ ೭ ೭ ೭ 3 ೭ A GIANT'S GRUMBLING

On the fourth day rain began, and it rained steadily after that. Vren hunched under his teba-cloth cape and the brim of his pointed hat. His good wool cloak was among the things missing from the house; and the teba cape, though it shed the rain, could not keep his shoulders warm enough. His long bear's-wool leggings kept his legs warm and dry, but his sandaled feet were wet at once, and cold, and stayed that way.

The boy's mood went dark and heavy as the sky. In the rain, Trim began to have more trouble finding the trail. Sometimes they had to go back along the same path, or scout round and round in widening circles until the spongy wet earth gave up a clue to him. Each time the wolf lost the trail, Vren thought it would not be found again. When it was, Vren felt no cheer. He thought only that they would lose it again soon and it would not, that time, be found.

On the sixth day, in the afternoon, Rusche's trail led them to a house, near the bank of a flooded river. It was a sort of burrow built half in the ground, with a low thatched roof made of bundles of horse-tail grass. No one was living in the house now, but no animals had yet pushed in the roof, and black sticks lay neatly inside the fire-ring, so Vren thought the house had not long been empty.

There was a strangeness in the air about that place, something that made him remember his own strong, dark feeling as he had come home to Rusche's empty house—and fear began to crawl inside his skin. If whatever thing had taken Rusche had taken this person as well, perhaps it was after all a giant, and Rusche these many days dead, gone to feed a giant's hunger. For the boy could not imagine any man or woman of the Under-Reach who would have the power and the cause to empty every house they came upon. He would not imagine that Rusche, himself, had emptied this one.

The boy named the river Ash, for its dark gray color— or perhaps for the burning up of his courage. This river, running now in flood, was many times wider than the White Stone. It moved very deep and dark and fast, sucking at its crumbly clay banks with a sound like a giant's grumbling. Rusche's smell stopped there, at the flooded edge of the Ash River.

Vren stood and watched the rain fall straight down onto the gray water. He liked to swim in the White Stone River. He swam well and carefully. And he had once seen Trim ambush an old broadbill duck by swimming silently below the surface of a lake. But the waters of the Ash raised in him a deep, cold dread.

Sliding past him on the river were limbs and rotted logs and full green branches of trees. As he stood watching, the water carried by the lifeless body of an opossum, its eyes dull and white and staring. A whole tree came as well, full-crowned and rooted, rolling heavily on the flood. He imagined the river's swift current carrying him and the wolf downstream as easily as if they were little leaf boats. He thought, if they were each able to reach the other shore, surely by then they would have become separated. They might be days finding one another, and then days more finding Rusche's old, rain-thinned scent —if it were there on the far bank at all. Perhaps Rusche had already drowned, like the opossum, his body carried away with the other debris of the flood.

Gloomily, the boy went a little way upstream and down, to be sure there was not a shallower place where he might ford the river. Then, because he could not bring himself to lie down inside the empty burrow house, he camped under a spruce tree with boughs that came down low like a tent all around the trunk. Inside, it was nearly dry, and the floor was soft, piled up with the tree's old brown needles. He could not have a fire there safely, and he was too tired and wet to look for something to eat. He only drank cold tea and ate a few bitter berries. And when the wolf went out to hunt, the boy lay alone and hungry under the tree.

The sound of the rain made him feel sullen and friendless. It came to his mind that Trim, in loyalty, should have stayed with him tonight, should have gone hungry, as he was. And then, slowly, he allowed himself to think of turning back.

There had been so few signs along the way—only a single footprint here, a scuff mark there—that it seemed Rusche might be deliberately hiding his trail. If not that, then perhaps the trail was hidden by the one who had taken him. And that gave the boy a different sort of fear. If he could find them at all, how would he overpower a man or a thing that had been strong enough to overpower Rusche?

Once, not very long ago, Vren had imagined himself and Trim defeating giants and monsters. But now, as he lay dismally alone in the rain, he imagined himself eaten by them, and Trim sent sprawling by the blow of a huge hand.

In the darkness later, he opened his eyes. He remembered no dream, but he remembered there had been one. His hands were sweating, though in the blackness under the tree it was very cold.

He lay awake and glum, listening to the rain, until there was enough daylight to see the tree boughs that were the walls of his tent. Then he went out and dug a few sura roots with a stick and made a small fire in the open, near the spruce tree. While he boiled the roots in his small dir-wood bowl, he sat with his arms around his folded knees and stared at the Ash River.

In a while, a thin spotted weasel came close enough to smell his foot, and he found he was glad of the company. He shared his sura with it, holding out a small piece on the palm of his hand.

But it was the weasel's willingness to come into his camp that made him begin slowly to worry. While Vren had been traveling with Trim, no small animal had come very near him. The wolf's presence had kept them away. Seeing this weasel now unafraid of the day-old scent of wolf, the boy began to think of how long Trim had been gone from him. He remembered times when the wolves had hunted all night and into the morning; but surely, knowing the boy waited alone, Trim would not do that today.

Finally, uneasily, Vren looked to see where the wolf had gone. In the muddy ground beside the river there were a few unclear tracks. Perhaps Trim had only come here to drink, or perhaps he had turned and trotted upstream or down along the riverbank. For lack of a clear sign, the boy set out downstream. He went as far as the second bend of the river. When by then he had still not seen any clear mark, he turned and went more quickly back to the beginning, to the spruce tent place. He thought he would find the wolf there, footsore and tired, curled up out of the rain. The empty space under the tree—so like the empty round house along the White Stone River, and the empty burrow here along the Ash —gave him a quick and frightening pain.

He began to search much more carefully and with much more fear. Along the upstream bank he found the tracks almost at once. There was the wolf's clear trotting stride showing in the muddy ground, and a little further he found a few long black hairs from Trim's coat, caught in the bristlecone of a young teba tree. So he went on upriver.

There were a great many deadfall trees. Where the wolf must have easily leapt them or trotted under them, the boy often found a need to climb or to crawl, so he did not go quickly. But he went steadily all afternoon without stopping to rest or to eat.

At dusk he reached a place where the river shore was flat and low-banked. Probably that place was damp much of the time: Cattails grew there in a thick underwood. Now the flood itself had spread out under the trees so the long brown heads of the cattails held themselves above the muddy water.

There was only a little daylight left, and the boy was not sure he could get clear around the flooded place to drier land before nightfall. But quickly he set out that way, along the edge of the swampy ground. His sandals made heavy sucking sounds as he pulled them free of the mud and set them in it again, one foot and then the other.

In the thick dusk, with his head down watching his footing, he heard the little whine, sounding not like Trim at all, but like some poor small frightened thing. He stood where he was and looked, narrowing his eyes against the lack of light. He nearly went on again without seeing where the wolf was, shoulder-deep in the deeper mud among the clumps of cattails. His coat, where it stood out of the bog, was muddy, tangled with twigs and leaves, dusted with cattail pollen. In the dim rain he seemed a limb of old wood, rotting into the mud.

"Trim!" The boy called the wolf's name once, quickly, in gladness, and then a second time—"Oh, Trim!"—in sorrow.

The wolf made a sound like a snapping of his teeth. He tried to lunge, as he must have tried for a night and a day, but in the mud his body only shook a little, roughly. His eyes were glossy with fever or with fear.

"Wait," Vren said. "Wait." His voice sounded too loud, and afraid. He pitched it lower: "Just be still. I'll get you out." He spoke for his own sake more than for the wolf, who would not know the meaning of the words but only the look that was in the boy's face, or fear if it was in his voice.

He put a foot out toward the wolf and let his weight onto it carefully. The ground swallowed his sandal and then quickly his ankle, with a sound like a popping of lips, so he pulled that foot back again. The wolf's eyes watched him unhappily.

"Trim," he said again. "I'll get you out." He had to try harder, this time, to make his voice sound steady and sure.

When he had thought a little, he pulled his teba cape over his head and spread it on the sticky black mud. Then he crawled onto it carefully, wriggling low without using his elbows or his knees. The mud squeezed between the fibers of the cape and slopped over its edges. It was cold as snow-melt against Vren's chest. But though he felt anxious and clumsy, lying flat that way, the cape held him as if it were a raft.

He knew he could not lift the wolf's great weight. He put one arm over the wolf's back and worked the fingers of that hand down into the mud under Trim's belly. The other hand and his shoulder he braced against the wolf's ribs. He hoped he might, at least, be strong enough to lever the wolf up onto his side and drag him backward onto the cape.

On one deep breath and then a second one, Vren strained. He heard the mud sigh a little, but he could not feel that the wolf had budged at all. In a moment he had to stop, to lie panting and shaking with his cheek resting against his own shoulder. As he lay that way, he could see the sorrowful look on Trim's face. The wolf held his muzzle closed and high, as if he stood in a rising water. With one yellow eye he looked at the boy, and waited.

In a moment, when he had his breath, Vren said, "I will get you out." His voice by now was high and out of control—and it was the third time, he knew, he had spoken those words.

He took a long hissing breath and tightened his arms, pulling at the wolf steadily, fiercely, with every muscle, every strength of his whole body, until he felt his face bulging, until he heard nothing but the pounding of his own blood inside his ears, and still on the one long breath, not giving way, until slowly, shuddering, the mud gave—and the boy's fierce stubbornness carried the wolf's big body suddenly right up on top of him. They rolled together in a jumble of muddy legs onto the firmer ground.

Trim thrashed weakly to his feet. He stood wobbly in shallow mud, his tail and hindquarters low. The boy was shaking, too. He sat up and put his forehead against the wolf's mud-slick chest, held the wolf's neck tightly without making a sound.

In a moment the wolf began to groom the top of the

boy's head, stroking the boy's muddy hair with his red, rough tongue. Slowly, then, Vren began to cry. They were scalding tears that ran in his mouth and into his ears.

He had not known until now, finding it again, that he had lost his hope.

ꙮꙮꙮ 4 ꙮ MIND'S EYE

They were tired and muddy and cold, but the boy's troublesack had been left at the spruce tent camp, forgotten on that bed of old dry needles. So in the darkness they picked out a path back around the flooded cattails, and then they simply lay down together on the first dry ground, huddled under the boy's muddy cape as if it were a roof. Vren slept with both his arms wound tight around Trim. And at dawn they started back for Vren's sack.

The distance seemed very much further than when the boy had come this way alone the day before. The wolf wobbled a little, setting his big feet down carefully among the roots and rocks. But slowly, by the walking, he got some of the strength back into his legs. Vren saw there was no illness behind his eyes, just his coat still flattened with black mud so he seemed bone-thin, as if he were sick or starving. Whenever they rested, the boy combed through the wolf's fur with his fingers, working out the stiff, dry mud, and gradually Trim looked himself again.

As they neared their old camp, with the boy following through the gray drizzle of the trees, the wolf stood suddenly still. He held his tail up in a high brush. In a moment, faintly, the boy smelled it too: the thin clean smoke of someone's campfire.

He tried not to think that it might be Rusche's.

He put his hand on Trim's shoulder, and they went on, more quickly now, until the boy could see the yellow fire, small as a candle's flame in the grayness. Someone had made a camp in front of the burrow house. The fire had been built before the open door, and a person sat just under the edge of the flat grass roof, looking into the flames.

Vren saw at once that it was not Rusche. The shape was small, almost as small as the boy himself. He squatted with Trim in the wet brush at the edge of the trees and watched the camp. He had learned from Rusche to take some care when meeting a stranger. But more than that, he had lately learned a little about being afraid.

The traveler wore a heavy hooded cloak with the hood pulled up around the head so the face was dark. Slowly, without knowing that he had done so, the boy decided it was a woman. She sat very still with her hands turned palms up on her crossed legs. Probably she waited for drier weather before she left the shelter. But it seemed to the boy as if she were waiting for someone to come, or for something to happen.

Vren tried to wait too, but he was very cold. Even his knees had begun to tremble under him. Finally he stood and, with one hand on Trim's neck, walked out onto the grass.

The woman, when she saw them, seemed only a little surprised, as if the two of them might have been what she waited for. She sat up straighter and lowered her hood. Then the boy could see it was the strange traveler woman he and Rusche had often met in summers, a woman named Shel. She had an uncommon face, round and dark and wrinkled as a po nut. When Vren had been younger, the woman's face had scared him. But she had always been polite and gentle in the times he and Rusche had visited her, so he stood still now and waited, as Rusche had shown him, for her sign of welcome or of refusal.

The woman looked from him to the wolf and to him again. Vren thought she might be afraid of Trim. He had seen, often enough, the way fear came up in people's eyes when they saw the red-back wolves. But if she was afraid, she kept it secret. Her face was only watchful.

She had no tea bowl the boy could see, but finally she

raised both her hands, open palmed, and said in a polite way, "Come far?" which was a traveler's greeting. So Vren walked slowly in to stand beside her campfire.

"So far," he said, in the traveler's way. His voice sounded dry and cracked to him. It had been a long time now, since he had spoken to another human being.

The woman gave him another of her slow, careful looks. If she remembered him from their few visits, she said nothing of it.

"Will you share this?" she said kindly, and reached up to him with a long-necked gourd bottle.

The boy drank a little from the gourd. It was a cold tea made from the leaves of raspberries. It would have tasted better if it had been hot, but he was glad to get it.

"Thank you," he said.

The woman seemed to think, and then she took a small hard lump of bread out of her troublesack and handed it up to the boy. "This too," she said, smiling just a little. "And sit down by the fire, if you please. You shiver like a mouse in the teeth of a big cat."

The bread was made of wild rice and water, and it was so hard Vren could not bite into it. He had to suck it and then grind at it with his back teeth. Still, he was very hungry and the taste was good. He drank more of the tea, now and then, to help the bread down. Trim sat back a little from the fire, but Vren crouched with his knees drawn up very close to the flames. He wanted to let the heat go all the way down into his cold bones.

While he ate, the traveler woman did not speak. She simply sat and watched him with steady eyes. The boy thought he himself ought to speak. He and the wolf were footsore and painted with mud, and he had not yet gotten his troublesack from under the spruce tree, so his hands were empty. Surely that was why she stared. But he could not decide how much to say, how much to leave out. Should he speak at all of Rusche?

The woman said suddenly, "The wolf was stuck in the river bottoms." It was not a question, so it startled him a little.

He nodded.

"Lucky you were strong enough to get him out," she said, as if he had told her as much.

And he answered, "Yes."

Her eyes still watched him, so that he felt more and more uneasy. It seemed as if her stare went inside his skull, a quick strange touch like an eyelash brushing the inner bone.

He stretched his hands out over her fire. "Do you know this river?" he asked shyly. "Do you know if there might be a shallower place to cross it?"

The woman shook her head. "I have not been on it before today. But the flood will ebb if you are patient. Or you might go another way."

The boy could not think of an answer to that without telling her the whole long tale of Rusche and the empty house. So he said nothing.

In a moment she said, "I had thought of weaving a little pillie-reed boat, myself, and going on down the river."

Vren had sometimes made his own small boats and sailed them, but they always let in too much water, or they were not quite true, and so went left or right and could not be made to sail straight. He thought, without saying it, that Shel had yet to find how hard it was to build a good boat, even one as simple as a pillie-reed canoe.

The woman began to smile, as if she had seen his doubt in his face. "I went across the Milk Lake, once, on a raft of my own making," she said. "And two days down the Horn River in a pillie-reed boat. Have not drowned yet."

Vren had never seen the Milk Lake himself, but people had told him of that place. The water was rough, and a fog lived there much of the time. The Horn River, like the White Stone, was rocky and cold and quick.

He ducked his chin a little, in embarrassment. "If you would not mind it, I would watch while you build the boat," he said. "I haven't ever made one that would sail true."

She simply nodded, still smiling slightly. Then, over

a long silence, she looked down at her hands and out at the trees. The lines of her face deepened slowly until there was something like a frown there.

In a low, raspy voice, as if unwillingly, she said, "Help me with it, if you like. We could be on the water, then, by morning."

There was a smaller silence, filled with Vren's surprise, for he saw he had been invited to share her boat. The woman lifted one shoulder, shrugging, but there was still a look like anger in her face.

"Your weight in the bow would give balance to a boat. I wouldn't mind if you went along with me a little way." Probably she thought his troublesack was lost, that he was alone, without even a tinder knife or a tea-bowl, and the cold season already creeping in among the bare trees.

Vren realized, suddenly, that yesterday or the day before he might have chosen to go with her. It would have seemed a better thing than returning, alone, to an empty house. Even now, he was afraid of the floodwaters of the Ash, and of what he would meet when at last he found Rusche. But finding Trim, he had found his courage again. Now he did not need to choose. He had already done so. He would ask Shel, in the little boat she would make, to take them across the flood, and then he would go on with Trim, along the trail of Rusche, until they had finally lost or overtaken him.

The woman spoke before he did. She blinked her

eyes as an owl might, slowly, and the boy felt again the eyelash touch of her stare. Then she said, in a new low voice, "You would as well go with me. The wolf, I think, will find no sign of your friend on the other riverbank. Probably he is one of those who has gone downriver on the Shadow-raft."

The boy felt a creeping of his skin, a prickling that went down along his spine and up into his scalp. The woman herself made a little, uncomfortable smile. She must have known she had frightened him, and by smiling hoped to make it less important.

She touched the edge of the burrow-house with her fingertips, rubbing the wood lightly as she ducked her eyes away from Vren. "There were eight who were here, days ago. Seven came, and when they left they took with them the one who had lived here, the dream-weaver, the eighth. One of the eight is a Shadow-shaper, and she has put the shape of a flatboat into mud and little sticks. They have sailed off in that thing, all of them, as if it were real."

In the silence after the woman spoke, the boy heard his own slow and heavy heartbeat. Seldom before this had he seen anyone's Shadow at all. There could be no pride in Shadows, among the thrown-away people of the UnderReach. Even Vren himself had sometimes gone away from a friend, turning quickly from a hawk or a shrew he knew well, and going off shamefaced when he thought someone might see them together. Rusche only rarely worked the weather, and never when he and Vren stood in view of others. No one Vren had met had ever spoken of a Shadow, or shown it, as this woman now did both at once, so strong and so awful—and he was afraid of her as he had not been of anyone since the day Rusche had stood over him, a wild-haired stranger. In fright he looked away from her, fixing his eyes in the trees.

She also carefully looked away. She said nothing. She only sat still, staring at her hands where they rested in her lap, as if now, like any other person, she had to wait for him to tell what he was thinking.

When there had been a very long silence, Vren glanced fearfully toward her again. Around her mouth and her eyes he saw a look he knew: the old, enduring pain of the one who is cast out. Suddenly, in his mind's eye, he saw his mother's face looking away from him, staring in unspeakable fright at the far straight edge of the sky—in the same way he now looked from Shel. Then slowly his fear of the seer-woman took a smaller shape, and slowly he began to think of what she had said of Rusche.

"Do you know where Rusche is going?" he asked her timidly.

He was glad the woman did not yet raise her eyes. "Probably there is not any plan in it," she said gently. "They are all following the spellbinder, and that one is aimless. He only goes where he likes and takes with him whomever he meets."

The boy shook his head. He felt suddenly braver, now that he was not believing her. "Rusche would not go off with one like that."

In a moment the woman said, low and flat, "I think the seven who are with that one would simply do as he asks, whether good or bad. He has hold of their souls."

Vren sat still, touching Trim now with one hand. Rusche, he thought, was stronger than that, and more true. But the woman's colorless voice frightened him again. *Not Rusche*, he wanted to say, but he could not quite speak the words out loud.

The woman's eyes came up and touched him lightly, so that he felt a chill. But she said, in a kind way, "There is probably no one who could stand against him. I have not seen or felt a Shadow as black as his. When I touched this house where he had been, I saw the shape of it as clearly as if he still stood inside it."

The boy hugged his arms against his chest. He imagined her touching this empty house and seeing, behind her eyes, some ghostly image of Rusche and of the spellbinder. And though he sat very near the woman's fire, he grew cold and shaky.

Stubbornly he said, "I don't think Rusche would go with him," and shook his head again. But he thought, more desperately, *Why would that one want to take him?*

The woman looked down at her hands again. She braided and unbraided her small bony fingers. It was a while before she spoke. Perhaps, as the boy had once done, she was thinking of how much to say, how much to leave out. Finally she answered the question he had not asked.

"Whatever Shadow belongs to each of those seven people," she said, "the spellbinder now owns it. From one of them, he gets a clear light, even in the darkness. From another, a boat made from mud, when he wishes to follow a river. His dreams, now, are woven as he likes. And no rain falls where he is standing."

Her eyes came up again, slowly, to Vren. Finally she said, "He is only dull and mean-spirited and selfish." As if that were reason enough.

ꙮꙮꙮꙮꙮꙮꙮ5ꙮ A CAT'S ANGRY BACK

In the morning, the boy and the seer-woman and the wolf traveled downriver together in their pillie-reed canoe. Trim was fearful of the boat, so the boy sat with him in the bow, one arm around his neck, as the woman with her long notched paddle pushed the canoe out into the river. Vren, too, was uneasy. But the woman quickly proved a good pilot. She kept the boat straight in the deep channel of the river, veering only a little, sometimes, to take them around rocks or fallen trees or the litter floating down with them on the flood. Often she used the paddle itself to push them away from a hazard. The notch she had cut in the end of the paddle always gave her a good firm grip, even on moss-slickened stones.

Slowly the woodland about them grew darker and thicker. The leafless hardwoods became fewer and the evergreens crowded in tall and straight and skinny, with all their boughs at the top. The forest here was like a huge high tent with many poles holding it up.

Under cover of those trees it was dry and dark, but on

the river, by midday it began to rain again, falling straight down from the sky above the boat. Vren hunched down under his cape and his hat and sat close to Trim for the little bit of warmth from the wolf. The woman pulled up the hood of her cloak, but she looked no more comfortable than the boy. Her cloak was made from the skin of an arad-elk. As it grew wet, it hung heavy and shapeless and cold from her shoulders. Probably later, when it dried, it would be scratchy and unbending. It was, Vren thought, a poor reason for the death of the elk.

He was now stiffly aware of all that came and went inside his head. Even as he thought this of the elk hide, he turned round to give the woman a shamefaced look. She only paddled on quietly without taking her eyes from the water. Vren wondered if it was with her eyes, only, or the touch of her hand, that she could look inside somehow or know a thing that had happened. And after that, slowly, he grew more at ease with her.

In the afternoon the river began to fall a little more steeply downhill. The clay banks narrowed and steepened, giving way at places to rock. Finally the boy heard a sound he knew from the White Stone River, the low steady growl a white water place makes. It echoed off the trees so there was no telling how far away it was.

The woman stood in the stern of the canoe, holding her paddle like a balance pole, peering ahead. From where he sat, the boy tried to look too, but the river bent and then bent again, out of sight. There were only poor places here to pull the canoe out of the water—the river ran quick and deep right up to its high mud banks—so the woman sat again and simply kept the boat straight and steady in the channel. When the boy looked back, he was glad to see her face was calm, and that her hands made a strong, neat grip on the dir-wood handle of the paddle.

It was only when they came around the second turn that the sound of the breaking water grew very much louder, and then they could see the narrow stone banks and the long white uproar of the rapids.

At once the woman's paddle cut into the water, and the bow of the boat swung sharply toward the shore. Then Vren saw, as she had, the only place where they might yet be able to pull the canoe out of the water. The river, in this flood or an earlier one, had taken a bite out of the bank, and in that little scallop the water was shallow and still.

Shel drove the boat crosscurrent toward it with quick, deep strokes. But the river, gathering its strength for the white water, took them on swiftly downstream. Vren, without pole or paddle to help her, sat uselessly a moment, clinging to Trim. Then, with his heart beating against his ribs, he took off his hat and his bulky teba cape, grasped the side of the boat with both hands, and slipped over into the river.

The current pulled his legs out ahead of him and tangled his long shirt around his thighs. Below the waterline, the slick curve of the boat started to slide from his grasp. He wriggled his fingers into the bundled, water-swollen reeds of the boat and began to swim hard, with whipping kicks, toward the shore. He could feel the boat move sideward a little, like the catching of a breath, with each of his strokes.

With his head down, braced against the boat, he could not see where they were. He could only hear the din of the water and Trim's fretting, snapping whine. So when the canoe lightened suddenly, he thought with a jump of alarm that Trim must have come in the water after him. Then his toes kicked the muddy bottom and he saw it was the woman herself who was wading chin-deep beside him, dragging the stern of the boat toward the near edge of the river.

There was no slanting shore, even here, but a steep cutbank of mud. Silently, panting, they struggled to get the canoe above it. Trim whined and fidgeted and finally gathered his haunches and leapt out of the jostled little boat onto the bank. Then they were able to pitch the canoe up onto the shore and climb up beside it.

For a while they only sat. The boy could hear the thin

shrill whistle of the woman's breath above the noise of the river. He himself was shaking with cold and tiredness and the end of his fear.

There would still have been time, probably, to scout a path around the rapids. The afternoon was only half-used. But he was glad when the woman stood and, without a word, began to build a rough bark lean-to.

Vren thought of taking the woman's carry-basket and hunting along the riverbank for the chain seed he had seen there. But she quietly heated her raspberry tea and brought out for each of them another lump of her hard, wild-rice bread—and the boy was afraid that he might belittle her simple traveler's food. He sat quietly with her in the early dusk and chewed at the bread and afterward was almost as hungry as before.

When the woman's eyes touched him in that small, flickering way—her Shadow look—he felt naked and dreadful. He was not very much surprised when she said, "I would have taken the basket, myself, and hunted along the bank of the river for the muddabs that live there under the stones. But I was afraid that might offend you." She was smiling a little, as she watched him.

Vren ducked his head from her and lowered his eyes. "They have not much soul, those little shellfish," he said in embarrassment. He did not tell her that he had sometimes befriended them, as he had the ant and the lowly worm. Perhaps she would see that, anyway, inside his head. He said, "Trim eats muddabs if he's hungry enough," so that she would feel free, like Trim, to get her own dinner, as she would have without Vren in her camp.

She still smiled a little. After a moment she made a small, soft sound that could have been a laugh, or a sigh.

"Anyway, I haven't the stubbornness, tonight, to get past those shells," she said. "I would rather pound a little chain seed and make a boiling dumpling." She handed him the empty carry-basket.

Her eyes seemed doelike now, very round and clear in that wide, wrinkled face. The boy saw suddenly why he could not stay afraid of her. Her kindness was there in her eyes, too, with the Shadow.

He took the woman's basket and went through the trees to the river. It was tedious work, stripping the chain seed pods by hand without a proper seed comb, but the basket slowly filled as the boy worked his way upstream in the dusk. When the last of the light was gone, he carried the basket back to the camp.

Between them, they had few tools. The boy had in his troublesack only the few things he had taken with him to camp among the bears, and the few more he had found at Rusche's empty house. Shel's troublesack was traveler-light. She had no proper tea-bowl, just one big wooden bowl for cooking, and the big plain carry-basket. She took a rock with a little dip in its top, and the blunt end of a tree limb, and with those tools ground the seeds slowly, a few at a time, while the boy heated boiling-stones on the fire and filled her wooden bowl with water. Then, from the seed-flour and raspberry tea and an old sprouted onion, the woman made a soft dough. Together she and the boy used notched sticks to lift the boiling-stones from the fire and drop them one by one into the water in the cooking bowl. The hot stones brought the water quickly to a boil, and into that boiling water, the woman put handfuls of her dough. The dumplings rolled and swelled in the steaming water, and sent out a pungent smell into the darkness.

When they had eaten the good, hot dumplings, the boy set to work by firelight, as he had the night before, picking the last of the black river-bottom mud from his cape. The woman quietly watched him, but not with her deep-seeing look. She seemed now just a plain-faced old woman, small and lonely, someone he could be-friend.

He had spoken seldom to any person other than Rusche, but he had listened well when Rusche had visited with others. So he knew he should not ask the woman to tell about herself. Instead, he said, "We have a small house above the White Stone River. You visited us there sometimes, in the summer. Do you remember? Our river has little white stones in its bed, like the blossoms on strawberry plants in the spring."

"I remember," the woman said, nodding without surprise. "Yours was the round beaver house under the teba trees. Once, I remember, we sat up very late talking. You were much littler then, and you fell asleep sitting up beside us. The weather-worker carried you off to bed."

The woman's words brought up in him a slow, melancholy ache, but she said, without seeming to read his thoughts, "It is a good place. You've put the house below the wind and above the flood line. And the trees hold off the rain. From the doorhole you can look a long way down the river's valley, in both directions. I thought, when I saw it, that someone had chosen that place very well."

Vren felt proud of his house, suddenly, as if he had chosen the site himself. He said, "There are soapberries all along the river there. And in the spring, red clover. The po nuts in the canyon behind us have thin shells because the little hot springs keep the air warm. There are good elbec fields at the Basket Meadows, half a day from us."

The woman's eyes widened. "I've been to that place, myself, for the elbec," she said. "I built a wintering house, once, in the lake country near there. From that house I could look out to a ridge shaped like a cat's angry back. Do you know where that is?"

The boy thought he remembered a ridge like that, near the Basket Meadows. It made him feel better about the woman, imagining her in an ordinary house not so very far from his own.

"You don't go back to the same house, then, in the winters?" he shyly asked her. There were many who wandered in that way, finding nothing and no one to hold them to one place. Once, in bad temper, Rusche had said, "They flee their own Shadows." But a few times, from anger or boredom, Vren himself had wanted to go.

"Every winter a different place," Shel said. "And no house at all from the spring to the fall. I have lived, so, for more than fifty years."

There was a tired unhappiness in her voice that made the boy look up from the combing of his cape. In his own short time traveling on the trail of Rusche, he had been too often afraid and gloomy, too often lonely and hungry and cold. Now, in the woman's face, he could see those miseries woven into each of the fifty years of her wandering. He could see them in the lines of her face as clearly as if he were the one with the seer's Shadow—and the very last of his fear of her disappeared.

He had not thought of it before, but now he said, "You are kind to help me find Rusche."

The woman ducked her chin. "Your weight balances the boat," she said, as if it annoyed her to be reminded of her kindness. Then, after a moment, she sighed and the irritation went out of her face. "Those eight will finally, somewhere, put ashore and leave the river," she said. "And I will let you out there, if we can find the place. After that, if you overtake them, that one will bind you to him, just as he has the weather-worker and the others. And that will be the end of you."

She smiled, but it was only a small curve that did not reach her eyes. "It is hard to find the kindness in that," she said.

The night before, lying awake inside his spruce tree shelter, Vren had thought endlessly of Rusche and of the spellbinder. He had slowly begun to wish that Shel had told him a tale of giants, or of great monsters with three heads and ugly, warty necks. When he imagined those things, he was only afraid. When he thought of Rusche going away with the spellbinder, his feelings grew dark and muddy. There was pain in them, and shame, and a different, more secret kind of fear. After a while he had begun to imagine that when he looked in Rusche's face, and said Rusche's name out loud, the man's own heart would unbind him. Now he sat very still and silent, not looking toward the woman. He was afraid, if he looked toward her, she might say something more. With only a few more words, she might blow the whole of his hope down around him, like a house made of leaves.

In the morning they carried the canoe around the rapids and set it again in the river, at a place where the water had slowed. The character of the river had changed. Often now there were white water places or short, rocky falls. They had learned, in the one lesson of the day before, to listen for the earliest sound of a rapids. Then, immediately, they pulled the canoe up on the shore. From there the woman walked ahead to look over the stretch of river that lay before them, and wherever she judged the water not too rough, they floated it.

Trim, squatting close beside the boy, shifted his weight anxiously with each shudder or wobble of the canoe, but the boy had learned to trust the woman's skill. Her paddle would dip quickly, easily, to one side and the other, sending the boat straight through, like a needle piercing cloth. And where she was not willing to risk the frail little boat in a thundering rapid, she and the boy carried it on their shoulders along the shoreline to quieter water.

In the afternoon, the river widened suddenly and

slowed, going out of sight between blunt, rocky banks. The woman backpaddled while she studied the gorge. Vren saw that, once between those stone walls, there might be no other place to get the canoe out of the water. Though he strained to listen, he heard only the low purling of the water under the bottom of the boat, no sound that might have been rapids. And finally, with a shrug, the woman let the current take their little boat into the canyon's mouth.

It was windless and quiet between the high walls. In the stillness there, Vren heard some small creature, perhaps a pocket mouse, or a dragon lizard, scratching its claws across a rock. He heard the woman's paddle dipping smoothly in the calm water. And it was only slowly that he heard the water ahead of them begin a steady murmur.

The woman stood sometimes high in the stern of the boat, yet for a while there was no white water for them to see. Even when the boat came past the last left-handed curve, and the water's sound rose up like a storm, there were no rapids. Instead, the river seemed wholly to sink and disappear, as though a great mouth drank it down. The cliffs on either side seemed to end there too, and beyond there was only the dull gray sky.

Even above the booming of the water, the boy heard the woman make a small sound of surprise, and then a grunt, as she pushed her paddle down hard into the water. He looked quickly back toward her, meaning to look for her small, strong hands on the handle of the paddle, seeing instead the alarm in her whitened face—and his fear rose up behind his eyes and made him blind.

Afterward, he only remembered the backstroke of Shel's paddle, like a quickened heartbeat, and above the din of the falls, the woman's voice—no words left in it, just the shout. He wanted to shout too, but by then, without his remembering when it had happened, the river had filled up his mouth.

The underwater was very dark and cold and bruising. Against his closed eyes he saw red star trails and then small winking yellow suns, but the only sound was the rush of the river in his ears. There was no getting up to air—he had lost track of which way the sky lay—but very quickly he did not feel afraid, he felt cold and heavy and far away from himself. He wondered if he might not be able to breathe the water, as a tayfish would, and as he had done, himself, in a dream. Finally, deliberately, he took the breath he needed, letting in the gray river's water, and then suddenly the stinging air, as he rose and sank and rose again, floundering across the angry backs of the waves. He choked and coughed up thin streams of water—and became again, very suddenly and clearly, afraid.

He could not remember letting go of Trim, but he was alone. There was no sign of the wolf or the woman or the pillie-reed canoe—only the dark, endless stands of trees sliding past on both banks of the water. Behind him, the falls had already gone out of sight with the river's turning.

"Trim!" He cried the name once, but it fell quickly and sank in the loudness of the river.

He kicked out hard with his legs, stroked with his arms, working across the current toward the far bank. His breastbone ached so he had to take air through his mouth in short, jerky breaths that burned in his chest. Very quickly his arms and legs grew heavy. His strength felt small against the power of the river, but he was not afraid of drowning, he was afraid to rest. He was afraid if he rested the river would take back whatever he had gained toward the bank, as every moment, steadily, it took him away from Trim, and from Shel.

He swam until his legs seemed no longer part of his body, but wooden sticks he controlled a little. His lips and his fingertips grew numb. Gradually, he began not to think of the others at all. He only thought of moving his arms and legs, driving his unwilling body across the water toward a sliding, endlessly distant line of trees.

When finally his knees beat into the gravel along the river's bed, he simply lay where he was, cold and sore, in the river's eddy. He sobbed air through his open mouth. He could not feel his tears except as saltiness and heat on his tongue. He could not yet find the strength to get all the way out of the water.

He wanted only for Rusche to come and wrap him up in a warm bear's-wool cloak and carry him home in his arms, as he had done when Vren was small.

6 ⊘ SO FAR

Alone and sore and shaking from cold, Vren found a way upstream along the bank of the Ash River. A few times he squatted at the river's edge and drank water from his cupped hands to fool his body away from hunger, but he did not stop to find food or to rest. He only limped a little more, and a little more, as the day and his strength slowly wore out. He walked on stubbornly, with his head down and his arms hugging the tattered pieces of his teba cape.

When it was dark, he lay beside a rotten log, with a loose piece of the log's bark pulled over him as if it were a blanket. A skrede must have had a burrow under the log or near it: After the boy lay down in that place, he could hear the skrede whistling its worries from somewhere nearby. It was too much effort tonight for him to befriend the little thing. He was too sore even to move. He could only lie wearily and listen to the scolding. Still, he could not sleep, shaking awake with cold and fear, and in the first gray light he began again, trudging upriver, until finally he reached the falls.

The cliffs stood up high and round, like the walls of a basket, and the water poured in. The boy stood in the loud, chill spray beside the pool. He stared. There was a little broken piece of the pillie-reed boat turning and turning in the white eddy there, but no sign of the wolf or of Shel.

In the dusk, in despair, he went back down the riverbank. He kicked apart every sodden pile of leaves or twigs lying in the shallows, in dread fear of finding a body hidden there. Finally, in the darkness, he simply lay down where he was on the damp ground. He did not think of anything at all. He only waited, without sleeping, for daylight to come again.

In the early morning, fog hung like the wings of giant snow-owls in the tops of the trees. In the stillness, the boy searched again through the crowded, brushy undergrowth along the riverbank. He called Trim's name out loud, and Shel's, calling and calling through the long white morning, though the river's endless roaring swallowed the words as he spoke them.

He found a place where he could walk rocks across the river to the other side, and he searched that bank as well. There he found his own troublesack, caught up in brush at the edge of the water. He pulled it dripping from the river and sorted through the few things inside. The star chart was torn, its old inks smeared and muddied. His tea-bowl was broken. Only his stone-bladed tinder knife was not ruined. He left the rest scattered on the ground there.

In the afternoon, Vren found a part of Shel's elk-hide cloak. There were dark stains on the hood that might have been mud, or blood. He left that scrap as he had left his sack, lying among wet leaves and evergreen needles. And after that he did not call anymore. He stumbled on without hope or thought.

The day warmed slowly, clearing out of the fog to a bright, dry sky, but at night the heat went quickly up into the stars and the grass grew crackly with frost. Vren might have been able to find a firestick tree and snap one of its small twigs to make a spark. But he made no fire and he hunted no food. He only wrapped himself in his teba cape and lay down on the cold ground. His burning, wide-open eyes stared at the darkness.

Slowly, and much, much later, he saw the fen-fox. How long had it stood, not more than a hand's reach from his face? It was small as a cat, with a cat's brushy tail, but no cat had ears as tall as the fen's turning each in its own direction, listening to two things at once. The boy had befriended a fen-fox once, when a rat had bitten its foot and made it lame. They were very shy and solitary. This one held itself stiff and ready, its trembling nose hearing what the boy must have said, in the unspeakable language of Smell.

Then, slowly, it brought its small face right up to Vren's. He felt its warm breath on his chin, speaking his name in the plain, unShadowed language of kindness. With its small raspy tongue, the fox began to stroke the boy's cheeks and eyelids, brushing out the muddy stiffness of his old tears.

The boy felt a stiffness go out of his chest, too. When the fox curled its small, warm body next to his heart, then at last he was able to sleep.

There seemed nothing to do but follow the river. Perhaps Trim or Shel or both of them had been carried further downstream than he had been. If not, then at least downriver was where Rusche had gone. If the boy could find Rusche, the two of them could go back upstream together to search for the others. Vren tried not to think of any other endings.

Though the fen-fox, after a while, went another way, the boy did not, that night, lie grieving uselessly in the cold. He broke a firestick and caught the spark in a handful of shredded bark. Then he blew gently into his hands until the smoking threads blossomed with flame. Crouched beside the fire, he carved a small rough dir-wood bowl with his tinder knife. In that bowl he could heat a little water for tea. The bowl was not large enough for cooking, but he chewed the long, tough roots of pinisap and ate the leaves of winter's-balm. He used a stick to grind nuts and seeds, and with sour vine-cherries for the juice, he made a thick nut paste to eat with two fingers.

For a time that night, he did still lie awake staring up through the trees to the pinpoints of the stars. Then a tree-skunk came to lie near him, as the fen-fox had, and in that quiet company he was finally able to sleep. The next day he made his way again, slowly, down along the Ash River.

Rusche's calendar string had been lost to the falls, so he kept count of the days with little scratches along the edge of his rough-carved bowl. On the afternoon of his fourth day alone, he came out of the trees into a wide clearing along the river's shore.

There had been a burn there once, from lightning or from a twig of firestick broken under some animal's foot. There were a few tall black poles of dead trees still standing on the open ground among pigweed and nettles, and one small, living, pinleaf tree. A spring of clear water came up out of the ground at the roots of the pinleaf. Close around that spring were crowded several little bark lean-tos, and a good stone house like the kin-houses the plains people built, with straight walls and a flat, tight-fitting roof.

The boy crouched at the edge of the clearing, staring at the house and the other rough shelters. He thought, with a jump of his heart, that it might be the camp of the spellbinder. Eight people traveling together would need several houses, as there were here, and Vren had never before, in the UnderReach, seen more than one house gathered in one place like this.

But he had imagined the spellbinder's campsite would have a feeling about it of danger and of secrecy. Not like this place, where he could see a big man doing the plain work of any household, carrying water from the little spring, putting sticks of wood on the cooking fire, stirring a bowl that smelled of pigweed and the flesh of some animal.

Vren thought the man must once have been strong. He had wide shoulders and large hands. But he had the look of someone who had eaten little for a very long time. His big bones were knobby and he walked stiffly, as if he were old and sick. The man came toward the boy, kicking through the long weeds looking for twigs for the fire, but though he came very near, he did not see Vren. His eyes were flat, and gray as the Ash River.

In a while, timidly, the boy stepped out into the open and waited for the big man to see him. That one's gray eyes seemed to look nowhere. He went on with his work slowly, without making any sign that he knew the boy was there.

Vren took a few more steps into the clearing. From the new place he stood, he could see a goat standing chewing at the pigweed beyond the furthest lean-to. There was a woman there too, sitting just under the edge of the little slanting roof. She sat with her knees drawn up under her chin and her arms folded around her legs. She did not look toward the goat, nor toward the big man, but off into the trees, staring. There was a dull look in her face, as there was in the man's, and that same thin sickliness.

While the boy stood there waiting, beginning to worry, another person came out through the door of the stone house. For one startling moment, Vren thought it was Rusche—the man wore a good cloak like the one Vren had helped him to make last fall, from the yellow bear's-wool—but this man was shorter and thicker than Rusche, with a soft round chin, dark eyes, a long balding forehead.

At once he looked straight toward Vren, as if he had expected to see the boy waiting there. His eyes were huge and black and glossy. He smiled a little, and then, so Vren might know he was welcome, he went to the campfire and put stones on to heat for tea. Invited finally, Vren found he was afraid to go into the camp. There was nothing quite fearful in the balding man's face, but the eyes of the other two made him uneasy. He wondered again if this might not be the spellbinder's camp, and thought suddenly of calling Rusche's name out loud, as he had once planned.

The balding man came toward him with a hand held out in a friendly way. He had an uncommon manner about him, bold and certain, as none were in the Under-Reach.

"Come far?" the man said. His voice was low, with a good furry softness to it, and hearing it the boy lost his thought of calling out Rusche's name.

"So far," Vren said. His own voice surprised him. The words came out slow and thick, as if he spoke from a distance, and not from within himself.

The man, smiling, kept on toward him. Vren thought of backing away, but his arms and legs felt slow, like his voice, and quickly the man came near enough to put his hand on Vren's arm. It was an odd, startling thing for a stranger to do, but Vren decided it fitted the man's bold manner—and the touch of the man's fingers was comfortable and very warm.

"Come in and share a little tea with me," he said. The sound of his voice inside the boy's head raised a light, pleasant humming, like a cat's purr. When he pulled at the boy's arm slightly, drawing him in toward the camp, Vren slowly went. He had lost his earlier fear of this place. Now he was only tired and lonely.

He sat beside the man, on a stump of wood near the fire, and gratefully drank the tea the man made for him.

Neither of the others came to join them. Those two still behaved as if they had not seen him at all, and rather soon Vren found that he no longer thought of them. The balding man's eyes, close at hand, were dark and bright as polished mirrors. Vren stared at his own reflection there. He had forgotten how he looked. He saw, for a moment, an unfamiliar boy with a wide, reddish face, bewildered eyes, a matted tangle of brown hair. And then he saw himself.

"We've been waiting for you," the man said, as if he were gently scolding. "The far-sighted girl beheld you this morning with her inner eye. I had not met anyone who could speak the languages of animals, so we've waited all day."

Each of his words rang slightly inside the boy's head. He felt light and giddy. He did not wonder who the far-sighted girl was, he had no curiosity about her at all. He thought of something else the man had said. He knew, suddenly, that he might call an archeagle to him if he wished to do so. He had only to open his mouth and that screeching voice would come out of his throat. *Kree-ee! Kree-ee!* There was only a little surprise in discovering this about himself. He could see it clearly in his reflection, in the dark eyes of the man. The boy he saw there had a great, wide Shadow, and Vren had, for the first time, no fear of it at all.

"I could show you," he said shyly.

The man smiled. When he did that, his eyes widened a little and grew blacker, and Vren had the dazzled sense that he had fallen into them. It gave him a breathless thrill.

"Speak to the goat, why don't you," the man said, in that gentle, slightly buzzing voice of his. "Just ask it to come and stand at your knee."

There was a cottony grayness at the edges of Vren's eyes. He turned his head carefully. The goat stood in a clear center of his vision, a small old nanny with a bony back and a dark, droopy udder. She had been staked to a rope, and all the weeds in the circle she could reach had been nibbled bare.

Oh. Poor old goat, Vren thought, forgetting archeagles at once in the feeling of this small thing's pain and loneliness.

He went to the edge of her circle, stepping slowly and carefully through the grayness. He wondered that he had not noticed this before: The many strong smells of her were like fine threads, twined together in a design as clear to him, now, as if it were a weaving he could look at with his eyes. It had been a long time since she had had a kid. The milk she gave now was thin and sour. She had nothing to eat here but pigweed and nettles, and no one to comb the burrs out of her coat.

The boy squatted so his face was level with hers. *Sweet,* he thought, in his old way, silently. He meant to say it, also, in the low bleating language of her kind, for he knew there was a goat's voice inside his mouth. But the goat he had named Sweet came at the first, wordless call. She stood beside him and put her furry chin on his knee. He petted her head, scratching along both cheeks until she closed her eyes.

"Ah. I'm glad we waited for you," came that pleasant, buzzing voice.

Vren had forgotten the man for a moment. Now he forgot the goat. He turned his head toward the sound of the voice, searching through the grayness, as a blind person might, until he had found himself again in the eyes of the spellbinder.

ⓔⓔⓔⓔⓔ 7 ⓔ WHISPERS

If the boy ate, he did not taste the food. If he slept, he did not remember the dream. Perhaps he moved slowly across a gray land, but he did not know the direction and did not see the sky. It seemed he may have carried a meaningless weight, or pulled it behind him, but his hands and his shoulders were only a distant discomfort. There may have been other shapes that moved near him, making small whispering sounds, but they were gray, and he could not see if they had faces. He had no interest in them at all. It seemed to Vren that there was only one other person in the world, and he waited, in the timeless whispering place, for that face leaning toward him from out of the grayness, or that voice, pleasantly droning, in his ear or inside his head.

At those times, when the two of them were together, Vren seemed to stand at the center of a cloudless place, in a small bright circle. Inside it, everything stood in clear, sharp outline, without confusion, like the treeless clarity of the plain. When he was with the man, he simply and truly knew the languages of animals. He knew, from Smell, all their small, important secrets, and heard their voices come out of his own mouth.

When he stood inside that bright space, he saw, in his reflection in the man's eyes, the great Shadow he cast. It was beautiful and splendid. And then he wondered how he ever could have felt fear and shame of it.

The boy held his hand out flat and still, and gradually the little woodmouse came and sat on his palm and examined the nit-seeds Vren had offered. The mouse balanced on his hindquarters and held a single seed in his tiny hands. He looked steadily in the boy's eyes while he gently bit the edges of the nit-seed's papery shell. The mouse smelled of dampness and wood-mold and rotted leaves and po nuts: He had made a nest in a cranny of a nut tree. His eyes were tiny and bright and black.

The man sat next to Vren, watching. After a while he reached out gently with one hand and closed his fingers around the woodmouse. Vren heard the tiny squeaking sound the mouse made. He would have shown a gentler way of holding. He meant to do that. But by then he had lost sight of the man's face, and in the thickening grayness he lost, also, the small prickly beginning of some nameless worry.

The boy and the man sat beside one another on ground that was soft and damp. The man leaned his shoulders against the rotten wood of a fallen tree, but the boy sat up straight, with his hands flat on the ground. He waited patiently. He felt clever and powerful and perfectly good.

In a little while, a thin black snake came and rubbed along his wrist. Its skin smelled of earth and powdery dry leaves and small stones: an underground den. In a moment the snake coiled around Vren's arm and lay still there, growing slowly warm against his skin. The boy stroked its throat gently.

It might have remained with Vren for quite a while, but the man, Vren's friend, moved stiffly in tiny ways, and finally the snake, with its tongue, smelled the man's fear and slid quietly away across the grass. Though the boy called it in the thin, whispery language of snakes, still it left the boy and the man sitting alone together in the twilight.

They waded in a river, and the boy pushed his hands gently back and forth through the water until tayfish came and began to rub their red-spotted sides against his palms. The boy's friend, in a while, put his hands in the water, too. Perhaps he caught his fingers in the ridged edges of a fish's gills—he jerked his hand as if he were startled, and the fish rose high in a spray of water beads and thumped out on the river's bank.

Vren felt, in his own chest, the tay's stunned fear. He meant to turn toward it, to help it again gently into the water, but the air felt thick and muddy. The man's hand was on his arm in a comforting way.

Vren stood on a rocky hillside among weeds that were tall as his shoulders. He could not remember how he had gotten there or where he had been in the moment before, but his friend stood beside him.

"There are red deer in these hills," the man said. "Can you call one to you?" His voice was low and buzzing so that the boy could feel it against his skin.

The red deer were voiceless, and their scent-glands were in their feet. He thought, if he simply waited and wished it, one would come to where he was. So he stood among the stiff weeds at the top of the hill. The man stood behind him. They waited and waited. The boy stood very still and patient. Finally a young buck with little stubby horns came out of the brush to see what it was that stood quietly and so long in one place.

The buck's eyes were round and clear. They made the boy think of someone else, though he could not find the face or the name.

He reached out his hand. The buck came and chewed at the fingers gently with small milk teeth. He had not been long away from his mother. In those wide brown eyes, Vren saw the deer's aloneness. He touched the deer's head, rubbing between the small, fuzzy horn-bumps.

Bloom, he thought, giving that name as a growing-up gift to the yearling. He remembered that he himself may have been alone once, but he could not remember any mother, nor the face of anyone else he might once have lost.

"It's a bright, beautiful Shadow you have brought me," the man said, in a thin whisper so the deer, Bloom, was not startled.

The man stood just beside Vren now. His hand was on the boy's arm with that good, warm touch, and Vren, at the man's words, felt light and soaring, like a water-sweet seed on the wind.

Then there was something at the edge of the boy's sight—a little movement, a small hushed breath of sound—and all the lightness went out of him suddenly, so that he felt heavy and sinking. A cottony grayness seemed to fill his eyes and his mouth, but for one moment he knew a clear and sharp alarm. He opened his mouth to say some word of warning to Bloom. The sound came out too slowly. By then it seemed to be only a small cry of confusion.

When he searched the grayness for the deer's trustful eyes, he saw his own small, dark reflection in the eyes of the man beside him.

. . .

A fen-fox came to the edge of some trees and looked at the boy. Vren heard the sound the man made, his "Ah . . ." of surprise and pleasure. The fen-fox was uncommonly shy. Probably the man had not, before this, ever seen the long burning-gold hair of that animal, its small fine face, great copper-colored eyes.

The boy remembered that he had befriended a fox like this once, or more than once. Slowly a sadness rose up in his chest, but it had no shape and no name, and in a moment it drifted out of him like smoke.

He squatted on the ground, with his hands resting open on his knees. The man did that too. Then, not moving at all and not speaking, together they waited for the fen-fox.

The boy thought of saying some word in the animal's own language. He was sure, if he opened his mouth, he could bring out the short, high bark of a fen-fox. But the fen had already left the trees and come a little way toward them, hearing some message that was silent, so Vren only waited, in wordless friendship.

The fox drew near to him. Her long, narrow nose touched the boy's hand. Then she put her nose close to his face, blowing warm wet breath against his skin, and he felt again something familiar, like sorrow. After a moment, the fen's rough tongue came out and brushed the boy's chin—and Vren remembered suddenly, all in a rush, the other time when he had lain grieving in the darkness below the falls of the Ash River, and another fen-fox had soundlessly spoken his name.

Something—the startled movement he made then, or the way his heart tightened up suddenly—something made the fen's eyes jump wide, and in the same moment she was gone, bounding away in long leaps across the grass and into the trees.

The man let out a word of anger. It was a sharp loud sound that echoed off the trees. There was one bright moment afterward. Vren saw the man's hard angry face, and his hand—the thin metal knife he held tightly in his fingers.

It seemed to Vren now, when he was with the man, that the space they stood in was very small. He could see it was circled about with wooly grayness that went out into black. Sometimes, standing in that small clear center, he could now hear the whispers of the gray no-time place, and it was hard to hear any animal's voice above that.

Now sometimes when Vren and the man stood together waiting, no animal came. Sometimes a snake would come, or a tree-toad, or a dragon lizard. The man wanted the red deer and the otter, but perhaps Vren had forgotten those languages. Or perhaps those animals now refused his friendship. The boy would stand impatiently waiting where he thought the deer might come, or he would open his mouth to call out in the squeaking sounds of the otter. But no deer came to where he waited, and nothing came from his mouth except the small, human sounds of his own voice.

In the man's eyes, when Vren looked for himself there, sometimes now he saw a small boy standing upside down. Or he saw himself standing alone, in darkness that seemed to go inward forever.

Without remembering that he had closed his eyes, Vren opened them. The man's voice whispered inside his head. The boy followed the voice through a shapeless darkness to where the man waited for him, sitting in a small, clear circle, inside the stone walls of a house. There was a light there, from no windows, but from the air itself. The boy could see the light reflected in the man's huge black eyes. It made the back of his head begin to tingle.

"Tell it to get away," the man said.

Vren had not heard it until now: a wolf's long, high howling from the nearby woodland. Then he could smell the man's fear burning inside the closed little room.

The wolf's voice only made the boy feel dimly unhappy. He said, "They sing a song like that, sometimes, to the stars."

The man's eyes grew very small, and the boy felt himself growing smaller too. "Tell it to get away," the man said again, in a rough, purring voice.

The boy had no memory now of the language wolves spoke, but he thought he remembered songs he himself had sent up into black skies. He put back his head and sang. No wolf's voice came from his mouth—he had only a boy's voice, after all—but he sang a high wailing star-song, a song without language at all.

There was a bright, clear silence afterward. Slowly the man began to smile, a smile that widened his eyes and sent the boy dizzily down inside them as he had not done in a while. But the wolf had not gone. His claws came scratching at the bottom of the door, his nose snuffling there, and the man's fear made the air in the room smell suddenly sharp.

The boy felt he had grown Shadowless. He could only stand and dully watch while the wolf splintered through the door. For a moment he saw the wolf clearly—the red ruff standing up along the shoulders, the long yellow teeth—and he smelled on its body old blood and sour breath of fever. He felt, or saw, the quick burst of the man's fear, too, and at that moment all the light left the inside of the house. It became as black as if Vren had no eyes, as if even his empty eye sockets had been filled up with blackness.

He heard a voice that could have been the man's, but it was only a high wordless whine inside his head, and the boy could not find his way to it.

The wolf's teeth closed in the hair at the back of his neck. He was not afraid of the wolf. But he folded up and tried to crawl away blindly along the ground. He was afraid that, inside the wolf's mouth, he was lost. For in this blackness there would be no finding his way down again into the Shadowed eyes of the spellbinder.

ও 8 ও BROKEN PIECES

He woke in darkness. It was cold, and his body ached as if he had fallen out of his high lookout tree into the shallows of the White Stone River. There was a small movement at his side, and he remembered something of teeth and blood and dark dream shapes. But this beside him was only . . . Trim.

He began to shake. He burrowed his face against the wolf's great chest, but even so, he could not stop the shaking.

"Vren," the woman said in a quiet way; and when he saw that Shel was there too, he began to cry.

"I thought you were dead," he said, now that it was not true.

He could not see her face clearly in the darkness, but he saw her lift her shoulders a little. She said, "When I came out below the falls, there was a big piece of the boat ahead of me on the water, and I caught hold of that and went downstream with it. Then when the wolf came near, I took hold of him by the neck and we got out of

the water together." She may have smiled. There was the
sound of a smile in her voice. "I followed the wolf some
of the time," she said gently. "And some of the time he
followed me. And we are here now."

Vren wanted to say again that he had thought them
dead. He wanted Shel to know what terrible days those
had been. "I found a torn part of your cloak," he said.

The woman was silent. Then for a second time, but
in a different voice, she said, "We are here now," and
he knew that these had been terrible days for them all.

They lay together, the three of them, among the
twisted black trunks of bare trees. The trees gave them
no shelter. They only made thin lines against the sky,
like cracks in a clay bowl. There was no sound at all,
here, not even a bit of wind to rub together the twigs of
the trees. It was a strange, silent country, colorless and
dead-seeming.

The boy did not ask what this place was—why or
how they had come here—but in a little while he had
to ask, "Have we come far enough away from him?"
because he could not yet quit shaking.

In the darkness he could see Shel's face watching him.
She answered slowly, telling more than he had asked,
perhaps to keep from saying yes or no. "We stopped near
his camp without knowing it," she said. "And when the
wolf cried, and you answered, I could not hold him.
He went off into the trees, and I followed him as best I

could, through the darkness. He had already brought you down to the edge of the camp when I came. So I carried you myself, into the ironwood. It is a dead place, and it seemed he might not want to follow us here. We went as far as we could. Until your weight was too heavy for either of us."

It made him ashamed, imagining himself carried like a sack of rocks, in Trim's mouth and across the old woman's shoulders, and suddenly more ashamed, re-membering the woman's Shadow-sight.

He had seen her once touch an empty house and then tell him of the people who had been there—even the shapes of their Shadows. Vren knew that, touching him, carrying him as she had, she might already know of Bloom the young red deer, of the spotted tayfish and the fen-fox and the spellbinder's long metal knife. She might have seen the gray, whispering no-time place, and the boy's reflection in the darkness of the spellbinder's eyes. If she had looked inward, all the way to the center of the boy's heart, she would know, as he did, what it was that made the spellbinder's Shadow so black. She would know that Vren, when he was with the spell-binder, had felt, for a little while, powerful and un-ashamed.

In the darkness, in guilt, he looked toward her. She was watching him. But in that dim light he could not see what was in her face.

They waited out the night, gathered close to one another for warmth and for courage in this cold, silent place. Vren did not sleep. He lay still, listening for the spellbinder, until the silence itself became a kind of sound—the long holding of someone's breath.

Only slowly did he begin to think of Rusche.

It made him feel feverish and sick, imagining himself and Rusche together in the camp of the spellbinder, not seeing, not knowing one another. He wondered if the wolf could drag a man big as Rusche down into the ironwood. If not that, how would he get Rusche away? Or should he try at all? For he could not stop shaking.

In daylight he saw that Trim was thin and weak. His black coat was dull, and the red ruff along his shoulders had gone dark, like muddy leaves. There was a long, scabbed wound along the curve of one hip, and another above an eye. He looked too ill to have dragged even a boy downhill from the stone house.

Vren looked dismally at Shel. "He is so thin and sick," he said.

The woman made a very small smile. "He and I were not the two who had been friends," she said, as if it were a reason. Then the boy understood. Shel said, "He slept and licked his wounds and ate grass, and he would not give me much notice. Twice I made a paste, from spidersweb and bloodroot, but whenever I came up close to him he . . . made a sound. And would not let me help him. A few times I caught mice. If I left a mouse near him and went away, sometimes he would take it. But most of that time I think he went hungry."

Vren was ashamed for her to know that he had wanted to send Trim, alone, to bring Rusche out of the spellbinder's camp. He touched the wolf's shoulder in apology.

Then, with only a little bravery, he asked, "Do you know the way back through the ironwood?"

He had remembered, by now, travelers' telling of an ironwood forest along one edge of the UnderReach, and so he knew what this place was. More than once, when he was younger, he had thought of going through the ironwood forest, or across white mountains, arriving Shadowless on the other side, at some other place. And during this long, sleepless night he had begun to think of it again, to think of going on into the ironwood without Rusche. But in the daylight now, and in guilt, he pretended he was not very afraid. He remembered that he had, after all, given warning to the fen-fox, and from the little hope in that, he drew a little courage.

Shel gave him a straight, long look, until he felt her eyes touching the inside of him. She must have seen his several secrets, but she only made a little sound, like a sigh. And then, slowly and in silence, she set off through the trees, leading Vren back toward the spellbinder's camp.

It began to snow a little as they reached the edge of the ironwood. Flakes of dry snow fell through the bare limbs of the trees and disappeared into the leaf-mold. They tried to move quietly as the snow. They set each foot down with care on the spongy ground. The last little way, where there was a scrubby underwood, they squirmed on elbows and knees below the brush.

The camp was gone. There was only flattened grass to show where the bark shelters had stood. A stony hill, grown with small hemmin trees, rose tall and untenanted, and behind that other wooded hills and a distant white line of mountains. The snow fell and melted among the little trees and the rocks.

"But—there was a pinleaf tree and a spring," Vren said, in confusion.

Shel gave him a small, gentle look. "That place is days from here. There have been a dozen camps since that one, I think. He stays only a little while in one place. When he has used up the wood and fouled the water and stripped all the berries and the small, sweet leaves close at hand, he simply moves his camp." She glanced at Vren. "And he took in another person after you, a woman who mends broken things with a touch. I found her empty house, in the trunk of a hollow teba tree, between the river and the ironwood."

Alone in the gray whispering place, it had seemed to Vren there was no passing of time. The small, bright moments he spent with the spellbinder he remembered now as if they were all one piece, like small round nut-shells strung together to make a single necklace. It had seemed to him that he had been in that place only a little while—a day, or less than that. It was a cold, cold feeling, finding all those days and places lost to his memory. Quickly the coldness settled at the center of his chest, making a weight as hard and brittle as ice.

Shel must not have seen it in his face. She stood and started up the hill without waiting for him. In a moment he made himself go up too. He was afraid to have her look back and see him still lying there, frozen.

They walked round the empty campsite with Trim, scouting out the trail to follow away from that place. In the grass, Shel found a clay bottle, broken in small pieces. Vren thought, if she touched a piece, maybe her Shadow-sight would be able to tell them the way to go. But he saw a slow dread come into her face, and she only stood and looked at the shards a moment and did not stoop to pick one up.

Vren felt he had not looked at her carefully until now. Without her great elk-hide cloak, he saw how very small she was. Her legs were short and bowed, and the hair at the back of her head was thin and yellowish and tangled. She did not walk in a bold, quick way, but slowly, sliding her feet through the grass. As he watched her, he began to feel at once more afraid—and more comforted.

The spellbinder's trail led them toward the far white mountains. Trim limped on a hind foot, and Vren himself moved stiffly and weakly, like the two people he remembered seeing in the spellbinder's camp, before he was taken. He saw, by his own bony wrists, that he had grown thin and pale in the lost days he had spent with the spellbinder. So they rested every little way, and often they took time to dig pinisap roots with a stick. They chewed the tough parts themselves, and fed the sticky inner sap to Trim.

Snow fell all day. The tiny, dry flakes disappeared as they touched the ground, but the air felt very cold. Vren wore his torn teba cape, and Shel had pulled a stiff cattail mat around her shoulders, but those clothes let the coldness through. When they sat to rest or to eat, they huddled close to one another, and stood again soon to go on.

Before dark, from the shoulder of a hill, they had an unexpected sight of distant figures moving in an unsteady line through the trees. From so far, there was no seeing faces, but they could see two of the people together pulling a sled, and a man riding on the sled as a sick person might—and Vren was pierced with sudden fear. That one, surely, would be the spellbinder. It would be foods and wooden cooking bowls and tools the others carried on their shoulders and in their arms— things taken from all of their houses.

Vren stood still, watching them. He remembered a weight he had pulled or carried across a gray landscape. And after all of them had gone out of sight, he stood stiffly where he was. He felt, if he moved, he might fall and be shattered.

Perhaps Shel felt something of that, too. She stood silently, hunching her shoulders, staring at the place where those people had disappeared. Finally, she said, "What can we do?" in a quiet, flat voice that frightened him. It made him think suddenly of her face in the moments before they went over the falls of the Ash River.

Since this morning, when Shel had stood small and old and afraid, looking down at the broken pieces of clay bottle, Vren had imagined her speaking in just that way, in a voice that said he should not go further. She would say, *There is no hope in it*, and then finally he would be able to turn around and look for a path home. Shel might even go with him. He would not follow the spellbinder, would not look for Rusche any longer.

But now the sound in her voice did not give him any comfort. It only made him begin to shake.

"The wolf cannot carry him out," Shel said in a dull, weary way. "We have not even the ironwood, here, to hide in. We would all be lost to him."

The boy looked down at the ground. All of his secrets had been shown to her already. He looked away because he could not bear to look in her eyes.

Shel watched him quietly a little while. Then, from inside her shirt, she brought out Rusche's calendar string and put it in his hand. She had tied several clumsy day-knots, to mark the time they had been separated.

"When the wolf had some of his strength back," she said, "I showed him this string I had found. I thought there might be your scent on it yet. And he would leave me and go to find you, if he could. I thought I would go back to a cave I had seen, a place in the high rocks near the falls, where I could make a good winter house."

She looked toward the wolf. Trim had dropped flat on his belly, resting beside Vren's feet, waiting for them. He did not look around to meet Shel's eyes.

After a little silence, the woman said, "I watched him go off downstream. Then he looked back to see if I was coming." She said this as if it had been reason enough for following. And now, not reason enough.

In a while he only asked her, "Are you turning back, then?"

She only answered, "Yes."

Without looking up at her, he said sorrowfully, "I

cannot go with you." He thought of saying something more, perhaps some word about the fen-fox, but it seemed too slight a thing, now, for hope. He waited, but she said nothing more. Carefully, he wound the calendar string around his neck and started down the hill, with Trim rising quickly to follow beside him. He went slowly, pushing his feet along through the wet, cold grass.

He looked back once. He remembered what she had told him, how she had followed Trim, but when he looked back, she only stood frowning at her feet, and would not watch him going away.

@ @ @ @ @ @ @ @ 9 @ A HIGH YELLOW FIRE

The boy and Trim watched from rocks along a hillside as the new camp was made. In the small valley of a creek, people leaned broken evergreen boughs against tree trunks to make three little shelters against the snow. One old woman slowly, with her empty hands and a few crooked sticks, began to shape the spellbinder's house.

The boy thought, *It is a Shadow!* He remembered the square stone walls, the tight roof, the door Trim had splintered.

Rusche was there among the others at the campsite. He was thin and frail. He had lost his pointed hat so his hair stood out in a tangled brush, and the red was dull with dirt. Vren could not see his eyes at all, below the thick hanging hair, but there seemed nothing familiar—nothing that was Rusche—in this man's soft mouth, his loose, open hands and hunched shoulders. Seeing him, Vren's heart stuck dry in his throat.

The sky came down low over the camp place. Rags of it were caught on the branches of the trees and the stiff, tall stalks of weeds. But the snowfall disappeared into mist above Rusche's head, and none fell on the sled where the spellbinder lay waiting for his stone house to be finished.

When the man stood up, finally, it was a surprise to remember how plain he was. He looked short and thick, next to Rusche. His dark hair hung limp behind a long bald forehead. Still, seeing him, Vren began to tremble. He wanted to close his eyes, so the eyes of the spellbinder might not find him. But he was not able to look away.

The man touched Rusche's arm and said a few words. From that distance, Vren could not quite hear what was said, and the voice seemed whining and thin. But when the boy saw how Rusche lifted his head and turned toward the sound—he felt a dark thrill himself, as if he heard the whisper of a low, buzzing voice inside his own ears.

He put his face down against the ground and folded both his arms up over his head. Trim's nose bumped against the back of his neck, but for a while Vren could not raise his head. He could only lie still with his face pressed against the grass, while the thickening snowfall settled on him like a cloak.

Before the door of the stone Shadow-house, a man and a girl built a high yellow fire. They dragged up long branches and bark pieces and carried in handfuls of twigs. Once the fire was built, the spellbinder came from inside his house and stood at the doorway, peering out into the darkness.

He touched the girl's arm when she came by him— and Vren imagined he could feel the heat of that touch on his own skin, going down to the bone. The girl's eyes found the spellbinder's face, and she told him something. Then the man looked straight up the hill to the place where Vren and the wolf lay watching. Vren could hear the sound of his own blood inside his ears. He lay utterly still, with his hand fisted in the fur along Trim's neck. If the man saw them, he gave no sign. He simply stared up toward them, and in a moment turned and shut himself back inside his house.

Now the boy remembered the far-sighted girl who had, that first time, told the spellbinder he was coming, and he knew this girl hauling wood must be the same one. Lying silently, crouched behind stones in the dark and in the snow, he felt all at once noisy and naked and unhidden. And all his hope went quickly out of him, leaving him flattened and empty, deserted even by tears.

Over the long night, the man came often to stand in the doorway of his house, staring out against the darkness. Several times he spoke to the girl, and then he would look toward Vren and the wolf. But slowly—as Vren lay in stiff fear holding in his own loud breath—

he began to see that the man's stare was blind, a searching frown, and always afterward the spellbinder would shut himself again inside his house.

So Vren slowly remembered the smell of the man's fear, how it had filled up the Shadow-house when the wolf had cried from outside.

And he knew that the man was afraid.

Vren waited until much of the night had run out, until finally he could not wait longer. Fear grew best at night, and it was the only weapon he had. He stood and took hold of the fur along Trim's neck and started down the hill. He meant to walk boldly in and lead Rusche away, trusting in the spellbinder's fear of the wolf to safeguard him.

His knees shuddered, not from cold. He felt the spellbinder must hear his heartbeat booming suddenly loud as any drum, but his feet, and the wolf's, made only a little sound, stepping through the snow. The wolf's shoulder, pressing alongside his leg, steadied him.

They cut a wobbly trail going down across the snow toward the camp. Vren had hoped the fire would be left to go out. In darkness, no one might see how thin and sick the wolf was. But all night the man and the girl had tirelessly dragged wood from out of the dark snowfall, and now, coming to the edge of the firelight, Vren felt his breath catch. It was Trim who kept on, pulling the boy beside him into the yellow glare.

The girl came toward them from beyond the snowsheds. Her shoulders were hunched with the weight of branches she carried. She was smaller than Vren, a chalky-faced little child. Vren stood stiffly, holding tight to the wolf, but the girl's eyes were flat and gray. She cast her wood into the fire and then wandered out again to the edge of the darkness. She did not look toward the two of them at all.

He watched her thin, stooped back going away from him. He had been careful not to think very much of these other seven who were with Rusche, but the girl's face, close at hand, let in a helpless guilt. The sound of his heartbeat filled his head so there was no room or calm for thought. He could only think that, afterward, when he was with Rusche again, he would be more fearless and more clever, and he and Rusche together might look for a way to unbind the others.

He came on toward the little sheds. He was not certain which one sheltered Rusche. He simply went to the nearest.

He had thought he should not look toward the spellbinder's house, but when the door of the house pushed outward, the movement startled him, and he looked without remembering that he should not.

The spellbinder stood in the doorway. The fire's light made a tiny yellow flame in his eyes. He seemed unsurprised to find Vren within his camp again.

He gave a simple traveler's greeting, as he had done another time. "Come far?" he said, in his low, pleasant voice.

The sounds set off a humming inside the boy's head. He stood still and watched the small fire burning in the man's eyes. He wanted to look away. He could feel his heart beating loudly, and he knew he should keep on toward the near shed, or call out Rusche's name as he had planned to do so long ago. But he only made a little, uncertain movement. A sound came up from his throat, but it was not a word.

The man smiled a little. He did not come to touch the boy's arm as he had done the other time. He stood where he was in the doorway of the house, behind the high fire.

"The far-sighted girl told me you were here. We've been waiting for you to come down and be with us again." There was a familiar tone of voice in the words —the sound of a friend's playful scolding. Slowly Vren could not think why he had not come down to the camp sooner.

"You look cold and wet. Come up next to the fire and get warm." The man stretched his own hands toward the fire, or toward the boy.

Vren was very cold. He remembered he had lain all
night in the snow. His feet were numb, and his chin felt
stiff. From where he stood he could not feel any warmth
from the high blaze. Dimly, he thought he should not
go up to the fire, but he could not think why. His heartbeat by now was slow and steady. And the man held out
his hand.

In a moment, with a little sigh of relief, Vren took a
step, and another, toward the bonfire.

Behind him something rumbled, a sound not quite
like far-off thunder, and he cast a slow, startled look
back toward it.

The wolf stood as near the fire as he would come. The
red hair along his shoulders had risen up on end, so his
head and chest seemed huge, and his long teeth showed
below his pulled-back lips. He looked past the boy to
the spellbinder. In his yellow eyes Vren could see suddenly and clearly the spellbinder's small, black reflection.

He felt his heart start again, with fear.

The man said, "Come up—" but by then Vren had
put his hands tight over his ears, and the words after that
had no shapes.

He pushed his feet toward one of the sheds. He felt
stiff and slow, and there was an itching inside his skull,
as if a little of the spellbinder's voice leaked through
his fingers, but he kept steadily on, with his back turned
to the man.

Under the first shelter there were people lying together in a pile, as animals will, for the warmth of one
another's bodies. They lay on the snow, with no mat or
covering except their own clothes.

A little of the firelight came inside, so Vren could see
their faces. One was the big man who had gathered
wood and tended the cook bowl when Vren had come
upon the spellbinder's camp that first time. Another
was a woman older than Shel. The knuckles of her
hands were swollen huge, and her fingers bent like a
hawk's talons. The third was another man, with sores
on his face and arms thin as little sticks. If they slept
at all, it was a Shadow-thing, for the three of them lay
with their eyes staring, wide-open.

Vren began to shake again. For a little while he could
not move away from there. He stared at the faces of
those three and, behind his own eyes, he saw the grayness of the no-time place.

But he could feel the heat of the wolf's body pressed
close to his leg, and he knew where he was and what
he would do.

He and the wolf went across the snow to the next
shed. Vren kept his hands pressed hard against his ears.
He did not look toward the spellbinder's house, but from
the edges of his eyes he could see the man still standing
there behind his big fire. He heard the wordless soft

rubbing of the man's voice still working to get inside him.

Vren bent and looked into the second shed. In the darkness there were two women lying huddled together, staring inward at the grayness.

He left them and went toward the third shed, where now he was sure he would find Rusche. He could not move quickly—the cold or his fear made him shaky and weak-kneed—but he set each step down stubbornly in a straight line across the snow, and he did not look toward the spellbinder at all.

He thought again of his early, childish faith, that the simple saying of Rusche's name would unbind the weather-worker; and before he had quite reached the place, he said, "Rusche," once, as if the word might be a charm after all. When he could not make it come out loud, but only a little whispering rustle, he felt a chill of foreboding.

At the edge of the shelter, he sat down heavily. It was empty inside. Snow had drifted up in a wave. He sat staring at the place where he had thought to find Rusche, and in a moment he let his hands drop hopelessly to his lap.

For a while his own sobbing breath kept him from hearing the spellbinder's voice; but then finally he did hear it, a vague soothing buzz inside his head. He had to stand on wobbly legs and look past the shed to the house.

A man, not the spellbinder, stood in the way between them. It was the man who had been helping to tend the fire, and now he let an armload of twigs and branches down onto the blaze. He seemed to watch the sparks showering up through the snowfall, then he went slowly away, out toward the woodland. And Vren could see the spellbinder standing behind the fire, with Rusche there beside him.

"You should come in to the fire," the spellbinder said patiently. Perhaps he had been saying that simple thing, over and over, while the boy had kept himself from listening.

Vren had lost his reason for staying away, so he started in, toward the fire. The wolf came too, pressing close beside the boy's leg. The man, without speaking, watched them come. There was a little smile around his mouth, as if he were not now afraid of the wolf. His fingers touched Rusche's arm.

The wolf again came as near the heat of the fire as he would, and then he stood still. The boy, whose hand rested on the wolf's back, stopped also. With great effort, he looked away from the spellbinder's eyes. He looked for Rusche, in the darkness below his brows, where his eyes stayed hidden.

Rusche, he tried to say, but he could not get the word to come out loud.

"Come round to this side of the fire," the spellbinder said. "Come here, and I'll give you my hand."

The boy felt a warm shivering that ran down his arm to the palm of his hand, as if the man had already touched him, but finally, carefully, he made a word come out of his stiff mouth: "No."

The spellbinder's eyes widened and then narrowed. Vren saw his own reflection flare and then grow smaller.

The man made a thin hissing sound, like a whisper. Then he did whisper, as if he told a secret. "You've missed being with me. It is only with me that you can truly speak in the languages of animals."

Vren could not, this time, make his mouth open. He could not say *No.* But he was able to stand stiffly where he was. He did not come round the fire to the spellbinder. In Rusche's blank face he saw the faces of the others, the ones lying under the cold snowsheds.

The man watched him. There might have been a little anger in the man's face now, or surprise.

He said very softly, whispering, "Will you come here and take my hand?" He reached out for the boy.

Vren closed his hands in fists and held them hard against his legs.

"Rusche," he said, in a small, hoarse voice, shaping the name finally, with pain and with care.

If the weather-worker heard it, Vren could not tell. It was the spellbinder who gave the boy, and then the wolf, a startled look: He thought the boy had spoken a word in the wolf's language. Probably he thought it a signal, or a command—and his quick fear must have sent its own command wordlessly inside Rusche's head.

The weather-worker lifted his chin. Then the boy saw his eyes, and saw they were not Rusche's eyes at all. The hair stood up on the boy's arms. Rusche's face was dark and terrifying and unfamiliar. When he opened his mouth, he let out a great, terrible breath, a dark billowing cloud, oyster-colored and huge and angry. The thing rose from his mouth and, with a long, heavy thundering, spread itself under the overcast sky.

Vren stood chilled and staring. Then, for only a little moment, he saw in Rusche's face a spurt of alarm, widened eyes, a look that made him think suddenly of the red deer Bloom, and the alarm he himself had sounded too slowly. His hands closed in the fur along Trim's neck. He tried to turn, pulling at the wolf—"Trim!"—but too slow again. The wolf stood stiffly, legs wide, his fur bristled, his lips curling back, even as the low Shadowed sky cracked open and let out its blinding white thunderbolt, and a boom of sound as loud and awful as the sound of the Gates slamming shut.

In the orange afterglare, Trim seemed to fly slowly from the boy, his body curling backward through a long, soundless time, while the boy was paralyzed, watching. Then there was a small sound, *whump*, as the wolf struck the snow. The air afterward was trembling and silent.

Vren could not cry. He could not get that much breath inside him. His chest felt collapsed. He found he was sitting in the snow himself, with his legs straight out before him. His burnt hands rested open in his lap. He looked from Trim to his hands in dull surprise. Then he looked at the spellbinder.

The man stood just behind the weather-worker's shoulder, in the doorway of the house. There was a look in his face, a little ugly boast. In Rusche's face, as if hardened there, stood a clear, single moment of startled grief. Seeing that, Vren slowly lost the need to cry. It leaked out of him quietly. When he had his breath back, he only sighed.

The spellbinder began to smile. He had smiled like that once before—when he had, for a moment, thought the wolf was gone, sent away by the boy's crying starsong. Now he stroked Rusche's arm in an absent way, without turning to see the look that was in the weather-worker's face. Then he left Rusche standing alone, and came around the fire to Vren. He squatted down so he could put his cold hand on the boy's shoulder and lean in near the boy's face.

Vren felt too tired and too sore to look away. But he

had lost, with the need for crying, the need for fear. In the man's eyes he saw himself, but pale and plain.

The spellbinder murmured in his ear. "Together again, you and I." His voice, inside the boy's head, was an ordinary man's voice, the voice of someone who was often afraid and always alone. "You have so beautiful a gift, in that Shadow of yours," he said.

Hearing it said finally, in a plain unShadowed voice, Vren knew, once and ever afterward, and with only a small feeling of surprise, that it was true.

Tiredly, he looked away. He looked for Rusche, still standing alone behind the high yellow fire.

"Rusche," he said, in a blurred and thin and childish voice, as he had used to call that name like a charm word from his sleep, in sure and certain faith the man would be there.

The spellbinder, at the boy's word, straightened in vague fear, and made a movement back toward the weather-worker. But he must have seen something in Rusche's face, or in Vren's. Perhaps he saw Rusche following his name back, finding himself in the eyes of the boy. For a moment the spellbinder stood unsteadily between Rusche and Vren. When snow began slowly to whiten his shoulders, fear and surprise came into his look.

The snow gathered in individual flakes in Rusche's

thick red eyebrows. It melted and hung in clear round beads, like rain or like tears, in his eyelashes. He made a slow, shuddering sound, and then he came toward the boy. The spellbinder put his hand on Rusche's arm, going past, but it was a short, shaky movement, a clutching, and Rusche flinched away from it and kept on, leaving the man standing uneasily alone.

When Vren had been small, Rusche had used to hold his hand sometimes, walking along a narrow or a steep trail. Sometimes Rusche had carried Vren on his shoulders or in his arms, sleep-sweaty and tired. That had been a long time ago. He had grown too big for carrying, too old for clinging. But now Rusche bent down for the boy, and Vren, beginning to cry, clasped his arms round the man's neck and climbed up, or tried to. He was too long-legged, too heavy, and finally Rusche staggered and knelt in the snow there and just held the boy against him, across his lap, their arms and legs tangled together. Rusche rocked a little, back and forth, and trembled, as the boy had done after Trim and Shel had carried him down into the ironwood forest.

"Vren," he said once, hoarsely and tiredly, with his mouth against the boy's hair.

The spellbinder watched them. He had a look in his face, now, like the one that had been in Rusche's, that same kind of surprised alarm.

ᘓ ᘓ ᘓ ᘓ ᘓ 10 ᘓ A SMALL CLEAR PLACE

There was a mark at the center of the wolf's chest, a blaze of singed hair. Vren stood back, with his eyes fixed on that small mark, while Rusche went across the snow to Trim. The boy's own chest felt weighted, as if the breath had been pushed out of him. Rusche stooped and touched the wolf. He slid both his hands over the rough coat, along the shoulders and the ribs and the thin flanks. When the weather-worker pressed a handful of snow against the burned place on Trim's chest—and Vren felt the flood of coolness below his own breastbone— then he saw the shallow rise and fall of the wolf's breath.

They carried the wolf heavily between them, to the shelter of the one empty shed. Rusche sat and held the wolf's big head in his lap and put his arm across the boy's shoulders. Vren leaned wearily against him. He looked out at the trees, and the steady, thick snowfall, white against the gray of daylight already coming up in the sky. But he felt the spellbinder's eyes watching, and finally he could not keep from looking toward him.

The man stood alone on the trampled dirty snow before the fire. He wore the big bear's-wool cloak that had been Rusche's, with his arms pulled inside so his head seemed balanced on a shapeless mound. He may not have been able to see Rusche's face or Vren's in the darkness under the lean-to; though he stared toward them, he seemed almost to look aside. A glittery brightness stood in his eyes, like unshed tears, or grief. Something familiar had gone from him, or something unfamiliar had come.

Slowly, the man who had been gathering wood came in from the pale edge of the trees. He waited there in confusion, blinking his eyes against the firelight, his empty hands hanging. The spellbinder turned his head and looked at him dully, without new surprise, as if he had, this time, expected to be betrayed. It was only later —as the far-sighted girl came shakily to the edge of the campsite, and one of the others, the big-boned man, rose unsteadily and stood beside one of the snowsheds—that he seemed at last to understand they were all unbound, as one thread, pulled, will undo a whole cloth.

After that, Vren saw his face slowly gathering malice and fear, until there was nothing of grief there, if ever there had been, only the shiny staring look that was not quite tears. Then Vren was able to see what was changed in the man's face. Perhaps the spellbinder had seen, in Vren's eyes and Rusche's, some small, true glimpse of himself—for his bright black unweeping eyes seemed to look only inward now, and in them Vren saw no one's reflection, only shades of night.

The man hunched his shoulders inside the heavy wool cloak, not shrugging, but protecting himself from some blow. He started heavily round to the stone house. Vren wondered if he meant to hide there, as he had done before, sitting alone in the exact center of the one square room. But the house had been abandoned. There were dark, cold gaps where rocks had fallen away, and little sticks stood in the openings, braced against the weight. As an untended house will do, this one became slowly unmade.

The man, when he saw the house, only hunched his shoulders again, as if he had not, after all, meant to go inside. He bent warily and reached through the door opening, snatching things to fill a troublesack: a bowl, a branch of firestick, the long, skinless red leg of an animal, poorly wrapped in a piece of rag. Then he turned and stood stiffly between the house and the fire, with the strap of the troublesack pulled up to one of his shoulders. Without quite meeting anyone's eyes, he cast a sort of bullying look out around the camp where several of those people were standing now, separately, shakily, at the furthest edges of the clearing.

There was a very long, waiting silence. He was only a short, plain man, in too big a cloak, and he was stooped a little under the weight of the sack. His eyes were huge and black, but it was only the small jumping flame of the fire that stood reflected in them. Still, in a while, the man with skinny stick arms came slowly forward. He did not look toward the others, but once, sidelong and deliberately, toward the spellbinder. Vren saw him narrow his eyes, in the way he and Rusche had used to do when they looked for shapes in the endless field of the stars. Perhaps the man drew, on the flat darkness of the spellbinder's eyes, his own bright, beguiling image of himself.

There were piles of things, of food and household tools, left carelessly about in the snow, and the skinny man began to rummage among them, filling a sack. In a moment, a heavy-faced woman with thick bare feet came after him, and began to gather things into her arms. Her mouth was stiff and set in a down-curved line.

The spellbinder watched them. Vren saw the look that came in his face, the little easing of his fear. When those two had taken up their loads, they came and stood a short way from him. They kept their faces turned down so Vren could not see their eyes. Then the spellbinder looked toward Rusche, or toward Vren.

"You see," he said, in something like his old, bold way. "Some of them will choose me." But his eyes were unglazed, flat, and when he spoke, his voice sounded small and shrill. It may have been the look in the faces of the other two that made Vren feel a last stirring, a shudder.

In a moment the man simply walked away from the camp, going quickly out of sight in the darkness under the trees. The two followed him, tramping behind, with their shoulders hunched and their eyes hidden. They left a heavy, broken trail in the snow.

Someone cried. Vren thought it might be the far-sighted girl, but then he saw her standing solemnly, with her thin bare arms clasped around her, and her lips pulled in to a flat line. Perhaps it was the old claw-fingered woman who cried. The high, thin wail made the air seem to shiver.

Rusche took in a little breath. He put Trim gently across Vren's legs and stood out of the shelter. Vren watched him cast about in the scattered piles of stores until he had found a deep boiling bowl, a few red onions and tuck roots, dried bunches of chai. He filled the bowl with cold creekwater, set stones in the burnt-down coals of the fire, and then, sitting on the snow, began deliberately to break the roots and the onions into the bowl in his lap. His fingers were long and thin, and they shook a little, so the dry skins of the onions rustled in his hands.

Snow fell quickly into the bowl and onto the sleeves of Rusche's thin shirt, and into the dwindling bonfire. For a little while he kept on as if the snow were not falling. He only shrugged his shoulders against the chill at the back of his neck. But then, without looking out at the others—only once, a small steady look for Vren—he set the bowl down and stood.

Vren knew suddenly what Rusche would do, though six people stood watching and there was, this time, no cross look, no shame in his face.

Rusche thrust his arm out once, cutting a wide, quick, impatient arc through the air. Afterward, from the small, clear place he had made in the snowfall, he looked out at the others, the people standing miserably, each of them alone, at the edges of the camp. It was only one look, sent round to all of them gently. Then he sat and took the bowl into his lap again.

In a little while, stiffly, the wood gathering man came within Rusche's unsnowing circle. He stood looking down at the collapsed center of the fire. Then with his foot he began to push in the unburned ends of wood, scuffing up snow and ashes a little, so the blaze whispered and spat. When he had gone all around the fire that way, he stood a moment, stooped and still, not looking toward Rusche. Then he went off silently into the trees. He came in again with two long wind-broken limbs. He fed them carefully to the fire, squatting down to place them each just so, and then finally sitting down himself, a little way from Rusche.

He opened his hands to the fire and rubbed the palms

against one another with a dry sound like the skins of the onions. There was a tired stare in his face, but it was unlike the stare of the gray no-time place. Once, shyly, he looked at Rusche.

After that they came in gradually, one and then another. Rusche's soup, when it was hot, went silently among them, the big bowl passing from hand to trembling hand. They did not quite look in one another's faces. But behind their eyes, Vren saw a look, sometimes, of old shared secrets. As if they had once, a very long time in the past, known one another as children.

When Rusche touched his ankle in the darkness, Vren woke and sat up from the warmth of his sleeping-robe. Rusche was already dressed for their going. He crouched on his heels next to the boy's bed, waiting. "Your face is still asleep," he said in a quiet, teasing voice.

Vren twisted his fists against his sleepy eyes. There were a few pale stars shining through the smokehole in the roof of their wintering house. By that star-light, stiff-fingered and cold, the boy tied up his leggings, put on a thick cloak, found his small new teba-cloth trouble-sack and the great teardrop shapes of the snowshoes he and Rusche had woven in the first days of winter, those first days after the spellbinder had gone.

Rusche went out through the low door, and the boy

followed him. They crouched beside the house, fitting their snowshoes, trying them quietly, tamping down the powdery drift in front of their door.

Softly Rusche said, "Tellado gave us these," and he put a few small rice cakes in Vren's hand.

The boy began to smile sleepily. He took from his own troublesack two flat patties of nut paste. "These are from Miesen," he said.

In the chill darkness, they stood together chewing the crumbly cakes and the pasties. The wolf rose up from where he had slept under the snow. He shook the loose white cape from his back and stood, sleepy as Vren had been. The boy nodded, yes, the wolf would go also. Then Trim worked the stiffness out of his hind legs, bowing low and stretching until his long muscles trembled.

In a little while it would begin to be daylight. The darkness had a thin look, like the water when you swim up from a lake bottom. Vren could see the white line of mountains against a far edge of the sky, and near him in the transparent darkness the several houses standing silently along the small valley of the creek.

A string of smoke came from the old Shadow-shaper, Uhle's log house. She took her sleep in short, scattered naps, to keep her swollen joints from stiffening. But the other houses were still and cold, their people asleep, waiting for the daylight. They had each of them, the night before, bid Rusche and Vren fair traveling, and safe return.

They set out quietly through the shallow snow. Their white breath plumed out, hanging still in the cold air behind them when they had gone on past.

The boy broke the trail. He remembered the way between the snow-cloaked hills back to the ironwood, and from there he and Rusche would be able to follow the wolf. Trim had grown restless and lonely over the cold season; he pined at night, in disquieting song, for his family. Vren knew, when the wolf saw the way they were going, he would begin to go ahead, eagerly finding the way for them back toward the White Stone River.

And when he saw they were not, after all, going all the way, Vren knew the wolf would go on alone, and finally home.

The sky filled up with clear winter daylight. Vren began to sweat, working hard, lifting and setting his wide-woven shoes in the snow. It felt good to be going, not thinking of much now except the careful placing of his feet.

The low hills seemed all of a kind, but coming up across the shoulder of one slope, Vren knew suddenly: This was the place where Shel had stayed behind. She had stood just there, alone, not watching him go away.

He had been thinking of her steadily, all these weeks. Rusche said she might have gone to spend the winter in the bowl-mender, Giel's, empty tree house, for that would have been the nearest good shelter. Or she had gone back to find that cave in the rocks, near the falls of the Ash River.

Vren and Rusche meant, themselves, to go that far, as they had used to go up the White Stone River to the Cat's Tail, to see the way the ice must hang in long fingers and fists at the edges of the water. But the distance, and the reason for going, were each much greater. Miesen and Uhle and the others would not look for their return short of twenty days. And when Rusche and Vren stood along the ridge between the ironwood and the river, at Giel's hollow-tree house, or later when they came below the falls, near the cave, they would search for Shel. Then, when finally they had found her wintering place, they would stand and wait patiently until she had filled up her tea bowl and set boiling stones on her fire. They would come in to share, quietly, their little bits of news: The six houses built together in the valley of Clear Creek.

Someone, in the first days, had called the place WintersCamp, where their houses stood all together, and so it was carelessly named, as if they would all go away from it in the spring. Sometimes, yet, one of them would speak of the place where their own old houses stood—telling themselves, or the others, they ought to go and live there. Vren himself still sometimes thought of the empty house along the White Stone River, remembering the thin-shelled po nuts and the color of the small rocks under the river's skin.

But the low hills at WintersCamp sheltered them from the wind, and the banks of the creek were thickly grown with jewel weed and moss, and whenever the clouds broke, the low winter sun shone easily through the bare branches of the hemmin trees, warming the roofs of their houses.

Vren thought, when he saw Shel, he would tell her those things, so that she might want to come with them and see the place herself. He would tell her that, in the spring, the hemmin trees would be putting on cloaks of lavender blossoms. And the air then would smell sweet and heavy with promise.